Gorgeous

Novels by Rachel Vail:

WONDER

DO-OVER

EVER AFTER

DARING TO BE ABIGAIL

NEVER MIND!

IF WE KISS

YOU, MAYBE: *The Profound Asymmetry
of Love in High School*

LUCKY

The Friendship Ring:

IF YOU ONLY KNEW

PLEASE, PLEASE, PLEASE

NOT THAT I CARE

WHAT ARE FRIENDS FOR?

POPULARITY CONTEST

FILL IN THE BLANK

Gorgeous

Rachel Vail

HARPER TEEN
An Imprint of HarperCollins*Publishers*

"An English Muffin (Is a Happy Day)" lyrics used by permission,
courtesy of Z & L Elkind.
"Constipation" used by permission, courtesy of H & E Fastow.

HarperTeen is an imprint of HarperCollins Publishers.

Gorgeous

Library of Congress Cataloging-in-Publication Data
Vail, Rachel.
    Gorgeous / Rachel Vail. — 1st ed.
        p.   cm.
    Summary: Ninth-grader Allison has always been the least attractive among her sis-
ters, but when she allows the devil to possess her cell phone in exchange for appearing to
be gorgeous, she must confront the power and deceptiveness of appearances.
    ISBN 978-0-06-089046-9 (trade bdg.)
    [1. Beauty, Personal—Fiction. 2. Self-esteem—Fiction. 3. Interpersonal re-
lations—Fiction. 4. Devil—Fiction. 5. Family problems—Fiction. 6. Models
(Persons)—Fiction. 7. New York (State)—Fiction.] I. Title.
PZ7.V1916Gor 2009   2008027468
[Fic]—dc22   CIP
                                                                            AC

Typography by Joel Tippie
        09 10 11 12 13 LP/RRDB 10 9 8 7 6 5 4 3 2
                              ❖
                        First Edition

TO MY GORGEOUS HUSBAND

1

I SOLD MY CELL PHONE TO THE DEVIL.

In my own defense, it had been a really crappy day.

The sun was in full show-off mode again, flattening our suburban town into a caricature of itself—rich, pretty, manicured. The lawns, the women, the girls my age: all manicured. Even many of the dads were manicured. Buffed, of course. No rough cuticles in our town. No rough anything.

"What a gorgeous day," people kept saying, as if they were revealing a wonder, and as if the gorgeousness settled an unspoken argument about our worth. "Absolutely gorgeous!" they agreed with one another. Mothers couldn't stop themselves from marveling out loud about the low humidity, the cuteness of each other's new sandals (and pedicures), the fact that our pools were all cleaned and opened already, weeks before Memorial Day. *Can you believe it? Oh, I know—I love it!* Knees and shoulders reemerged, fake-tanned to perfection, tulips and roses mingled condescendingly with the so-yesterday daffodils, and only a few of the puffiest, whitest clouds accessorized the sky, punching up its cornflower blue.

I was finding it hard to breathe.

Beyond even the migraine-inducing falsetto chatter about the shocking fact that in these days of holes the size of Texas in the ozone layer, it could be—gasp—warm in the late spring in the New York suburbs, my fascist social studies teacher had started my day off by being a complete hypocrite and giving me a B– on my paper. I completely couldn't give a rat's butt about grades, honestly—it is my older sister Quinn's job to bring home straight A's, not mine—but I had for once actually put in some effort, and the only comment on it at all was that I had not gotten my concept approved.

Which was a lie.

We'd submitted our concepts three weeks earlier. The assignment was to write about someone who had changed the course of world history. My best friend, Jade Demarchelier, was doing Eleanor Roosevelt; Serena Smythson, who was apparently not allowed to choose to study Jade, who would obviously have been her first choice, was therefore also doing Eleanor Roosevelt. Leonardo da Vinci, Beethoven, Gandhi, and Shakespeare were other popular choices. I'd chosen to study Gouverneur Morris, a one-legged drunken carouser with multiple mad and murderous mistresses, who wrote practically the whole damn U.S. Constitution including the famous "We the People" section, despite the fact that he thought only *some* people (meaning rich people) could be trusted to self-govern. My thesis was that this "genius exotic" won power for the people in spite of his aristocratic worldview. I still had my thesis statement paper, with the Fascist's two-word comment, the only one on that paper, in her tight-script purple ink: *Interesting! Approved.*

So when I got back my paper on Gouverneur Morris with not one correction on it but only the words *Unacceptable Thesis! B–* scrawled across the top of it, I was beyond pissed. I marched up to the Fascist and said, "Excuse me, this thesis WAS approved."

She tried to argue, but I shoved the thesis statement paper under her beady eyes. She relented but then started arguing that there were "other problems, too."

She wouldn't say what, though I have a feeling she was referring to the section about his housekeeper/mistress who was accused of murdering her illegitimate child. But the Fascist said, "End of discussion," an expression I seem to be allergic to because it sends me into fits of rage, and that is why I ended up tearing my report on Gouverneur Morris into tiny bits and hurling them at her face.

It is unclear who was the most shocked person in the classroom as the flakes of my report fluttered down over the Fascist's head. The Fascist seemed pretty shocked.

She may actually have been *in* shock, judging from how she froze, other than a slight tremor throughout her body. Or it could have been Jade, who would never ever talk back to a teacher, never mind throw stuff at one, and who stood there staring at me like I'd just sprouted a second head. But I think it might have been me, honestly, especially when the Fascist didn't scream or send me to the principal's office or anything. She just sat there, shaking slightly, allowing the scraps of my report to cling decoratively to her frizzy hair.

It was almost festive.

When the Fascist turned to talk with one of the nicer kids, I walked toward the classroom door. I could see Jade turning to whisper to Serena. I swallowed hard and kept walking, out into the hallway.

"You okay?" a girl named Roxie Green asked me.

"I hate everything," I answered.

"Let's cut second period," she suggested.

"Okay," I said.

She didn't look surprised at all. I myself was by then totally blown sideways. And not just because I'd never cut before.

We walked out the back entrance of the high school and wandered around a bit. We didn't really know each other that well, Roxie Green and I, so we didn't have much to talk about. She had moved out to our lovely suburban patch of hell from New York City over the summer. She lived on my street, down a bit toward the corner, in two houses—one of which, supposedly, was being converted into a rec house: indoor pool, squash court, yoga studio, the works. The rumor was that her family was the richest in our town, which is saying a lot. Some people said Roxie had been a model in the city and the real reason they moved out was that her parents wanted to get her away from the wild life of clubbing and drugs. She looked like a model, that was for sure—tall, thin, and gorgeous. Jade and Serena and I had been eyeing her all year for signs of wildness, critiquing her hair (strawberry blond, very straight, jagged edges), makeup (lots of black eyeliner), and clothes (kind of out-there, weird combinations of pinks and reds, and lots of bracelets).

If she noticed nobody was really talking to her, Roxie didn't show it. She didn't seem to care. She didn't seem to give a crap about anything.

"There is really nowhere to go here, is there?" Roxie murmured.

"Absolutely nowhere," I agreed, checking around and behind us. I wasn't sure if maybe there were security officers, watching for cutters. But even worse, if Jade saw me cutting second with Roxie Green, she'd definitely give me the silent treatment.

"You live down my street, right?" Roxie asked.

"Yeah," I answered. "Welcome to the neighborhood, belatedly."

"Thanks. It sucks."

"You noticed," I said. "You must miss the city."

"You have no idea how much." She pushed her hair back from her forehead with her pinky and thumb. "You know why we moved?"

"No," I said, kind of telling the truth. What I knew was only rumor. "Why?"

"Can you keep a secret?"

"Absolutely," I said. "It's the only good thing about me."

"It's kind of embarrassing," she warned, watching my face. When I didn't flinch, she whispered, "My parents had a sudden urge to garden."

"Ew," I said. "How hideous."

She looked at me with her head cocked, and then nodded. "Beyond hideous. Let's have a pool party."

"Sure," I said. "When?"

"Today," she answered, pulling out her phone. "You know Tyler Moss?"

I'd had a crush on Tyler Moss since September. Once, just before February break, while pretending to look for my sister Quinn in the tenth-grade hall but actually stalking Tyler, I impulsively said hello to him and he hit me with his mitten. I was psyched out of all proportion.

Kind of pathetic, I admit. Jade knew I loved him, but nobody else did. Not even Serena, who would've told the whole school.

"Swim team?" I said, trying to sound blasé. "Dark hair?"

"That's him," Roxie said. "Bring a few friends," she said, and texted at the same time. *Alison Avery and I are having a hard day. Come cheer us up.*

"It's two L's," I told her, feeling like a dork. "A-L-L-I-"

"I thought you needed a nickname," Roxie said. "Alison for short. Do you already have a nickname? Allie or something?"

"No," I said. "Well, my mom called me Allie Cat a couple times when I was little, but I hated that. My dad calls me Lemon."

"Why?"

I shrugged. "Sour personality?" She looked horrified, so I added, "He means it in a loving way, I'm pretty sure."

"Oh." We kept walking. "How about Alison with one L?"

"Yeah," I agreed.

Her phone buzzed. Tyler Moss had texted her back saying only, *Excellent.* Roxie showed it to me and smiled, her dimples deeply indenting her cheeks.

We wandered back toward school as I spilled the whole story of why I'd torn up my paper and thrown it at the Fascist. Apparently it was hilarious in the telling. Roxie's laugh bubbled up and then boiled over, making it seem like I was the funniest, wildest person she'd ever met.

Jade stalked up to me in the hall as soon as she saw us round the corner. "You weren't in math," she whispered. "Everything okay?"

"Yeah," I said, and then realized I meant it. "Everything's great."

"Is it?" Jade raised her eyebrows. "I don't want to be late for French." She hurried away with Serena, as always, in her shadow.

"She's a real party," Roxie said, and despite the fact that Jade was my best friend, I felt myself smile a little.

"She's just serious," I explained.

"I don't get it," Roxie said. "You're so fun and she's, like, the tightest girl in the school. Why do you hang with her all the time?"

"Um," I said, thinking, *I'm fun? Seriously?* "I . . . she's . . . we're, like, practically cousins, for one thing."

"You are?"

"Family friends, you know? We always used to rent houses together, Augusts, Fire Island . . ."

"Used to?"

I shrugged. There wasn't a nonobnoxious way to explain that we'd stopped doing that a few years ago, when Mom got her hedge fund job and my family moved to the way nicer section of town and started renting August houses, just us, in Europe.

"Whatever," Roxie said, strolling down the hall as I scurried to keep up.

"We have a lot of history, Jade and I," I said, feeling again like a total dork—but what was I going to do, explain that, although Jade sometimes drove me nuts, nobody else was exactly chasing me around school begging to hang with me, and a person has to eat with *somebody* at lunch? Can you spell loser? So I mumbled, "Plus, she's smart, and . . ."

"Uh-huh," Roxie said, sounding unconvinced.

"She is—and loyal, loving . . ." How weird to be defending the perfect Jade Demarchelier, my own personal Jiminy Cricket, so patient with my cranky selfishness she was practically a saint. "We've been best friends since kindergarten. You get used to her, and then she's great, really."

"She's an acquired taste?" Roxie asked, turning down the corridor toward French.

"Yeah, maybe," I agreed, worn out. "I guess so."

"I don't really acquire tastes," Roxie said. "I still hate grilled eel, and bourbon."

"Yeah, well." I laughed. "I never thought of Jade in quite that company."

"Sometimes a new person sees clearer." Roxie held the door open to the French classroom and whispered, "Seriously. Eel. Bourbon. Trust me."

Madame gave us a slightly dirty look as Roxie and I tumbled to our desks, cracking up while the bell rang. Jade's expression was much more disappointed than Madame's. I had to turn away because that scowl of Jade's actually did make her look a little like an eel who'd sipped too much bourbon, and I was on the verge of peeing in my pants, thinking that.

After French, everybody moved in a blob toward the cafeteria, and for the first time, Roxie sat with me, Jade, and Serena. It was weird. Roxie was the only one who talked at all. I mostly nodded and tried not to smile.

By seventh period, Roxie had convinced me that the *excellent* from Tyler Moss earlier in the day had some possible reference to me.

So after school, I had to go dashing home to have a bathing suit crisis as fast as possible, while denying completely to my older sister, Quinn, that I had cut despite the fact that she apparently saw me sneaking back into school at the end of second period.

I let my younger sister, Phoebe, help me choose a bathing suit, because she is beautiful and popular and irritatingly cheerful, so she would know which bathing suit would look good. Also, she is very honest—so if one suit made me look dumpier than another, she would tell me. I yanked an assortment of possibilities out of my closet for her to evaluate.

She chose my new black-and-white print. I pulled on my cutoff shorts, my low-top sneaks without laces, and a loose tank. My hair is impossible, so I didn't even bother doing more than pushing it in front of my weird face, to cover as much of my alien-looking eyes as possible.

Over Easter weekend, my grandmother had said I was "interesting-looking." Sweet, right? How clear was it that she meant "ugly"? Especially after she had just been going on and on about how lovely and refined Quinn had become, a classic beauty with such porcelain skin like you never see, and how much Phoebe looked like Mom, so vivacious and getting prettier and prettier every day, before she spotted me and added, "Now Allison, she is more . . . more *interesting-looking*." Great. Thanks, Grandma. Subtle. I left my chocolate bunny in pieces on her kitchen counter when it was finally time for us to leave.

What a treat, to spend my life between the two pillars of perfection that are my sisters. Joy! Delight! Ain't life grand?

And yet as if I had never met myself, I went la-di-da across and down the street to Roxie Green's, like something lovely might happen with half the boys' swim team gathered at her magnificent pool.

Not having thought to bring his mitten in the 85-degree heat, Tyler Moss completely ignored me, preferring instead to join with his three best friends, one more hard-bodied than the next, in a flirt-fest with the stunning Miss Roxanne Green.

Roxie laughed hard over something one of the boys mumbled. They all laughed along, too.

I almost went in the pool for something to do, until I remembered my hair looks even worse after a dousing.

Bored and lonely with only well-muscled backs to look at for entertainment, I was about to doze off until one of the boys accidentally sat on my leg. Emmett O'Leary. My existence had not registered in his consciousness, apparently.

"Sorry," he said.

"Doesn't matter," I said.

Well, that was a lovely interaction.

Then I had a soda. Also nice. Ooh, what a delightful afternoon.

My cell phone buzzed with a text from Jade:

What was up w/ u 2day?

I texted back:

Just another perfect day in paradise.

Meanwhile, Roxie, trying to open up the conversation to include me, said, "Oh, you guys! You have to hear what Allison did to the Fascist today!"

"Who?"

"That's what Allison calls what's-her-name, the social studies teacher with the hair? You know?" Roxie held her hair out to the sides and grinned, her dimples deepening their incursions into her cheeks. The boys laughed appreciatively and never moved their eyes from Roxie's gorgeous face.

"Tell them," Roxie encouraged me.

Unfortunately I started back a little too far in the story, because instead of being impressed with what a badass

I was, Emmett O'Leary got kind of stuck on what state was Gouverneur Morris governor of, and it turned into a comedy routine of *Oh, I thought you said he was governor/ No that's his name/What's his name/Gouverneur Morris/And what state did you say* . . .

Tyler cracked up, but it was more *at* than *with*. I knew Roxie was trying to throw me a line and rope me into the conversation. I knew she was not intentionally hogging the attention of the four boys practically panting for a smile from her. It was just a fact of her life.

I stood up and said I had to go. Nobody objected. I walked around Roxie's house down to the street and toward home, answering Jade's next message

where r u?

by texting back

hell.

Phone in hand, I passed three other houses, all well tended, all perfect-looking. *This is where I live,* I was thinking. Right here in hell. Right here, where if you are not gorgeous, you are nobody.

U OK? Jade texted back.

I don't even exist.

??? was all she responded.

Sorry, I typed with my thumbs. *Weird attack. I'm dandy.*

I stuck my phone back in my pocket. It was running out of power anyway, the piece of crap. I trudged home, feeling completely nonexistent, which is a much heavier sensation than it sounds like. *I would give anything,* I muttered to myself (or at least I thought it was just to myself), *to be somebody.*

2

AFTER SUCCESSFULLY DODGING my nosy, annoying family by barricading myself in my room, I read for a while, cleaned out my desk, scrubbed the plunger for my costume in the morning, then found the old baby monitor Quinn had asked me about because she needed it for some project she was doing. It was on the top shelf of my closet. I dropped it on her mess of a desk while she was downstairs practicing piano.

I spent ten minutes doing my normal half-decent minimum on the night's homework, and then tried to find something to watch on TV. Nothing. Jade texted me (*we have 2 talk*). *Ugh.* I held the phone in my hand for a full minute, gearing up for the onslaught, trying to think how to minimize the problem.

Instead I turned off my phone. I knew she'd be way mad and there'd be a price to pay in the morning, but I just couldn't deal right then. What I really wanted was oblivion, so I crawled into bed and flipped through one of Phoebe's ridiculous fashion magazines. I took half a quiz about *Does He Like You?* (he didn't; shocking!), learned the diet secrets of an actress I'd never heard of (drink lots of water; fascinating!), and eventually bored myself into a stupor deep enough to knock myself unconscious.

I thought I had woken up a few hours later, but maybe I was still dreaming, because there on the couch in my room was the devil, his long legs crossed, his long arms crossed, and his green eyes not crossed, but rather focused on me with only the slightest expression of impatience.

Not that I believe in the devil. Obviously. I don't believe in anything.

It was just a dream.

It must have been a dream.

He leaned back against the seat cushions and said, "So, you'd give anything for your sister Phoebe's metabolism?"

"What are you talking about?" I asked him.

"You called this meeting," he said.

I normally have no problem arguing, but I was a little off my game because of still trying to focus my eyes properly, so what I asked (instead of, for instance, Who are you? or What the hell are you doing in my room in the middle of the night?) was, "When?"

"Well, today you said you'd give anything to be

'somebody.' Two days ago, before you burned the waffles, you told your younger sister, Phoebe, that you would give anything for her metabolism."

"She burned the waffles, not me," I argued, kind of missing the main point, but I honestly cannot stand getting blamed for Phoebe's screwups, which I always do. And the burned waffles were all her.

"Okay," the devil conceded.

"And I was kidding," I added.

"Were you?" He arched his eyebrows. He barely blinked his green eyes, looking at me.

"Yes!" I said. "I swear, I was completely kidding!"

"Alas," he said, but made no move to go.

"Sorry to waste your time," I added.

He didn't budge.

I needed to go to the bathroom, but I was only wearing a thin T-shirt and boxers. Even though I was dreaming him, and I kind of knew it even in the dream, I didn't think I should, like, expose myself.

To the devil.

Who I was dreaming.

I pulled the blankets up around me and started getting the giggles at the strangeness of the situation.

He cocked his head, interested.

"I don't normally have such vivid dreams," I explained.

"Ah," said the devil.

"Were you, like, going to trade me Phoebe's metabolism for my soul?"

He didn't answer, just kept looking at me.

"Do people actually make deals that are so lopsided?"

"Lopsided?"

"Her metabolism isn't even that awesome," I pointed out.

"Okay," he said.

"Would she, like, get fat?"

"If that's important to you, we could negotiate it," he said.

"It's not!" I told him. "I was just curious! But seriously, for my soul? A slightly faster metabolism? Would anybody make such a stupid deal?"

"Why do you think it took me two days to come?" he said slowly. "There's a wait list."

"Oh my God," I said.

"No," he answered.

"Oh, no, I mean, I didn't . . ."

"Kidding," he said, with a smirk. "So what *do* you want?"

"As a trade for my soul?"

"While I'm here . . ."

"I don't even think I have a soul, I should warn you. I kind of suck."

He smirked.

"Oh! You already know that about me, right? I mean,

18

is that, like, part of your job?"

He cocked his head slightly; since he looked more intrigued than annoyed, I went on.

"I'm nasty and jealous and very sensitive, if you believe my sisters. I'm totally selfish. And cranky, too. So I don't know why you'd negotiate for my soul at all. I mean, if you exist, and if *it* exists, neither of which I am convinced of, by the way, you'll definitely be getting my soul eventually anyway."

He nodded. "Eventually. But you could have something now, if you want it. What do you want, Allison?"

"Oh, that's easy. To be gorgeous and brilliant and maybe immortal—no, wait, I shouldn't be so selfish, right? How about a long, happy, healthy life for me and everybody I love, world peace, and a million more wishes."

"I'm not a genie."

"Oh," I said. "Right. No million more wishes?"

"No," he said. "I'll give you gorgeous."

"Sell my soul to be gorgeous?"

He shrugged.

"But then I could, like, die within a day of turning gorgeous, or something."

He smiled. "Very good. Okay, you'll be gorgeous, and you'll live at least a normal life span, unless you do something crazy like lie down on the train tracks or start smoking or something. I won't kill you off early just for spite."

"Awesome. Thanks," I said. "But how about if I give you something else? Instead of my probably nonexistent soul."

"Oh?" he asked. "What have you got?"

I looked around my room. "TV?"

He shook his head. "Mine's nicer."

"Tennis racquets?" I pointed at them, lying beside him on my couch. "You can have them both. They're brand-new almost, top of the line."

"I play golf," he said.

"My cell phone?" I offered.

He didn't budge. I wasn't sure if he was hearing voices from, like, the underworld or something. I listened but heard nothing.

After a minute he said, "Let me see it."

I picked my cell phone up off my night table and tossed it to him. He opened it, pressed a few buttons, turned it over and over again in his big hands. "The camera doesn't even have a flash."

"So what?" I said.

"Midlevel cell phone . . . gorgeous." He held my phone in one hand and, I suppose, my imaginary gorgeousness in the other. Apparently my imaginary gorgeousness weighed significantly more.

"I could, like, spread rumors about how cool you are, plus the phone," I offered.

He squinted slightly at me, which crinkled the corners

of his eyes. He was actually a hottie, despite being, like forty, and also imaginary. "I'm not in the market for a new PR rep," he said. "On the other hand, I like you, and I like the springiness of the keys on this phone. And I'm already here. So. Tell you what. Choose somebody, and that person will *think* you're gorgeous."

Tyler Moss immediately sprang to mind, but I altruistically countered, "What about the whole world-peace thing?"

"You don't even get decent Internet on this," he said, using both thumbs and making my phone beep and buzz like it had never done before.

"Fine, I don't have to *be* gorgeous. Everybody can just *think* I'm gorgeous. Come on. It's apparently got a ton of ring tones . . ."

He scrolled through my phone book. "Isn't seeming gorgeous the same as being gorgeous?"

"No," I said.

He smiled to himself. "Damn close, though. Fine, choose three people who will forever think you are gorgeous."

"Ten," I countered. "The keys are so springy."

"Five."

"Eight. I already lost a cell phone once this year," I explained. "If I have to go to my mother and say I lost this one too, she'll give me hell."

He grinned, looking up from the phone.

"No offense."

"On the contrary; I'm flattered." He held the phone toward me in his open palm. It looked tiny, lying there. "But you won't have to tell your mother anything. You'll have the phone. I'll just *possess* it."

"Isn't *having* the same as *possessing*?" I asked.

"No," he said.

"Oh, the other kind of . . . Right. So I'd keep the phone?"

"Yes," he agreed, his arm still outstretched with the phone resting in his big hand. "And I'll meet you in the middle. Seven. Seven people will think you are absolutely gorgeous."

I got a little distracted, is my only defense. Seven is obviously closer to eight than to five. *I won* is what I was thinking when I said, "Deal."

He said, "Deal," and disappeared, or else I just stopped dreaming about him. Well, whatever. I woke up the next morning having forgotten about it completely.

Until my cell phone started freaking out.

"Lemon!"

My eyes flashed open as Dad knocked on my door and added, "Rise and shine!"

I saw my clock and started cursing.

It was too late for a shower, which I desperately needed. It was also too late to figure out a better costume for my presentation or, obviously, a change of topic and thesis for my end-of-year twenty-percent-of-my-grade social studies project. Not that I was ever considering dumping Gouverneur Morris, my one-legged slutty brilliant hideous hero, but still. As if it's not bad enough to have my paper (another twenty percent of my grade) dissed by the teacher in front of the class yesterday—well, and then shredded by me—I now had to present it, in all its B– glory, to my whole class.

In costume.

As the one-legged hideous slutty genius himself.

A normal person (Phoebe) would have done somebody easy. Actually, Phoebe would probably do a movie star so she could go in looking even more beautiful than usual. Quinn did Galileo last year. She just wore her hair in a bun and held a pendulum. She had hers totally memorized, of course, having practiced it in front of Mom and Dad a thousand times.

Not only was Jade's Eleanor Roosevelt costume perfect, she even had a great bonus prepared. I had helped her make little business cards to hand out to everybody after her project with a quote: *"Do one thing each day that scares you." E. Roosevelt.* Did I have handouts? No. I had a plunger.

"Why didn't you wake me earlier?" I yelled to anybody who was listening. Or wasn't.

I whipped open my closet to find my loose brown cords and the white blouse I had "borrowed" from Quinn, who sometimes does dress, luckily, like an eighteenth-century guy, all frills and velvet. Usually just for piano concerts, but I am convinced she actually enjoys it.

"Who took the plunger?" I screamed, when I realized it wasn't beside my couch where I'd left it. "I need the plunger!"

Dad wandered by with some crack about stuffing up the toilets. He thinks he's such a guy, so laid-back and cool.

"It's for my costume, dude! I have a project today?"

24

If it had been Quinn's project, the whole family would've been expected to be gluing cardboard buckles onto wingtips, but since it was my project, it was obviously a joke.

"Where the f—"

Before I could finish, our housekeeper, Gosia, was at my door with the plunger. I grabbed it from her. "I left it here on purpose," I told her.

Gosia raised one perfectly tweezed eyebrow and tiptoed silently away toward the back steps, down to deal with lunches. She totally favors Phoebe. Maybe it's a straight-shiny-hair/perfect-skin/skinny-girl-bonding thing. Or that Phoebe doesn't scream at her. Not sure which.

I'd had an idea about doing a ponytail-flip thing to make myself look more like Gouverneur Morris, but my hair, like the rest of my life, was refusing to cooperate. I had the scissors out from under the sink and in my hand before I talked myself down off that crazy ledge, reminding myself of past horror shows that were the result of self-induced haircuts. I tucked the huge mass of it all into the cap I had taken from Dad's closet. It was completely anachronistic, but would have to do because Dad didn't actually own any tricornered hats. Or if he did, they were all in the kindergarten classroom where he is king and jester all rolled into one.

I made my bed, straightened my room in three seconds flat, and flew down the back stairs to hit the kitchen just as Quinn was threatening to leave without me. Gosia thrust a disgusting nutrition bar into my bag as we left.

"Are you seriously getting on the bus with a plunger?" Quinn asked.

"You are so mean," I said. "It's my peg leg." I tried to demonstrate but almost fell over, and had to jog to catch up to her. "The bus isn't even there yet."

"And where's your hair?" she asked.

"Am I repulsive?"

"Yes," she answered.

"Awesome," I said. "Thanks. After I spend the night finding your crap for you."

That got her attention. "You found the baby monitor?"

"I left it on your desk!"

"Oh," she said. "I didn't see it."

"Maybe if you ever filed a paper, you'd—"

"Shut up, Allison," she said.

"What kind of project are you doing with a baby monitor, anyway?"

"Nothing."

"I don't see what you could make for chemistry with a baby mon—"

"It's not for science, okay? Jeez, Al, you almost touched me with the plunger."

"Sorry!" I held the plunger down. We were steps from the bus stop and, of course, no bus in sight. She always worries we'll miss it, so we're always there way early. "So then, why did you need the baby monitor? To spy on some-body?"

"Yes," she said.

I stopped arguing, stopped swinging the plunger, stopped everything. "I was kidding," I said. "Are you?"

"No," she said.

Quinn is the most straight, moral person who ever walked God's green earth. She doesn't curse or cheat; she doesn't even whine or complain or eat ice cream right from the container. She works hard and plays by the rules. She flosses, for goodness' sake. She would never spy on any-one. "Who are you spying on?"

"You can't say anything."

"You know me," I said. "I would never tell; you know that."

"True. Okay. Mom and Dad," she said.

"Oh." I wasn't sure if I should be relieved or disap-pointed it wasn't me. "Why are you—"

"What was that?" Quinn asked. "Did you just turn your phone off?"

"No," I said. "You paranoid spy. That was yours." But when I grabbed my phone out of my pocket to check, it was off. "Weird," I said, and tried to turn it back on. Noth-ing.

"Maybe it's dead."

"I charged it last night," I started to protest, but then it turned back on by itself, in my hand.

"You just have to hold down the thing for three seconds," Quinn instructed me in her slow-talking way that makes it sound like everybody is stupid except her.

"I know," I protested. "Why are you spying on them?"

She rolled her eyes but leaned close, like the trees might overhear. "I heard them arguing last night, and then I heard Mom tell Dad that . . . Allison!"

My phone turned off again, making its loud sign-off music.

"Will you quit it?" Quinn demanded impatiently.

"I didn't do anything!" I told her. "Oh! I know what happened! I had the weirdest dream last night. I sold my—"

"Allison," Quinn growled. "I honestly don't give a crap about your dream. Do you want to know what I think is happening with Mom or not?" The bus was finally screeching and jolting its way down the hill toward us.

"Yes," I said quickly, slipping my phone back into my pocket. "Of course. Chill, would you?" She is always telling me to chill. She is the most chill person in the world. Normally. It was odd—and, I have to say, sort of great—to be the one telling her to chill for once.

Quinn took a breath and leaned close. "Last night I heard her arguing with Daddy about—"

She interrupted herself to glare at me. My phone was beeping inside my pocket.

"I'm not doing anything!" I told her. I yanked the phone out again and showed her what was happening on the little screen: It was scrolling down a list of options I didn't even know existed on my phone, choices of modes like Outdoor and Pager. I tried to get it to stop, but it wouldn't.

"It's dying," Quinn diagnosed.

"No," I said. "I sold it to the devil."

"Forget it."

"Fine, don't believe me," I said. "You are so nasty. Do I look different today?"

Quinn shook her head and exhaled, without really looking at me.

"Seriously," I said. "Do I?"

She looked. "You're wearing a hat," she said. "And holding a plunger."

As I was hitting her with the plunger, the bus squealed to a stop in front of us and farted. While we waited for the doors to wheeze open, I tried to catch a glimpse of myself in the reflection from the windows. I couldn't really see anything conclusive. Not that I expected to. But my phone was squawking in my clutch again, so I was kind of cracking myself up by thinking, *Maybe it really happened.*

Quinn got on ahead of me and made her way up the aisle to where the tenth graders were sitting. I plunked down in my usual seat, three back from the driver, and stared out the window. Jade and Serena were waiting at the next stop. I could see them as we came over the hill.

The bus screeched and jolted still. I looked up. Jade looked at me and then away. Serena did the same. Instead of sitting down with me, Jade took the seat in front of me, and Serena giddily bopped down beside her.

So that's how it was going to play out. I should have known there'd be the silent treatment. Maybe I had known. You don't suddenly throw your report at a teacher and cut a class with the wild new girl and, worst of all, turn off your phone and then just go back to normal. Not with Jade.

I was on my way to first period, alone, when Roxie bounded up and grabbed me, talking before I could even listen, telling me a long, convoluted story about how she missed the bus as always because, this time, she'd been tearing through everything in her parents' closets coming up with a costume since 6 a.m. She was laughing straight through the telling, so I missed some of what she said, but I had to smile anyway, she was enjoying herself so thoroughly. We were almost at the door of social studies when she interrupted herself with a gasp.

"Why do you look like that?" she asked me.

"I'm Gouverneur Morris. Didn't the Fascist say you couldn't be a fictional character?"

"Who's changed the world more than Harry Potter?" Roxie demanded, shoving her wire-rimmed glasses, octagonal instead of round, up her nose. "Man, I can't see in these at all." She whipped them off and stared at me. "No, seriously, Allison. You look different."

"Hat," I said. "Plunger."

"Hot," she argued.

"Really?" I asked. "Um, can I hide behind you? I have to lose half a leg."

"Sure." The bell rang. Roxie spread her arms to turn her mom's poncho from Harry's robes into a makeshift changing room. I had to scrunch low and hide inside Quinn's blouse while I pulled down my pants to wiggle my right leg out, bend it, and tuck my foot next to my butt. Then, while barely managing to zip my squishy pants, I stood up and stuck in the plunger, plunger-side up, all the while praying nobody had used the thing since I'd scrubbed it the night before. I was in a soaking sweat.

The Fascist picked on me to present first, probably as revenge for having been confettied, so I was in a total sweat as I limped up to the front of the classroom.

Maybe that was a good thing, though, because I forgot about the fact that my best friend was totally glaring at me and that I hadn't gotten around to memorizing my paper. I just acted pissed off and superior and told the first-period ninth-grade social studies class about my (well, Gouverneur Morris's) theory that only the aristocracy could be trusted to run the country, but that, at the same time, yes, I was the one who wrote the preamble to the Constitution, starting with "We the People" rather than, as some of the twits in the Constitutional Convention had wanted, "We, the Several States of the Union" or some uninspired

31

crap like that. And I further denied categorically that all of my mistresses were murderers, insisting that not even a majority of them ever killed anybody of note.

It was fun.

After I finished, nobody said anything. I just stood there and suddenly felt off balance, awkward, humiliated, and sweaty again. "Whatever," I said. "Anyway, that's it."

Then Roxie started clapping, and a few other people joined in. Including the Fascist herself. Not Jade, though. No way.

"Wow," the Fascist said. "Allison, that was, well, remarkable. That is, I felt I was listening not to a ninth grader reciting a report, but to this historical figure as a real person." She squinted at me.

I could tell she was thinking maybe Quinn had written it for me or performed it for me or something. Maybe she was trying to figure out if Quinn had actually come to the class dressed as me dressed as Gouverneur Morris. "What?" I said, yanking the plunger out of my pants leg and knocking myself off balance into her desk.

"Excellent," she said, and turned to the class. "That will be a hard act to follow. Who's feeling daring?" she asked them.

I couldn't get my leg free, is why I had to ask to go out into the hall for a second. It wasn't because I needed to recover from the shock of getting a compliment from the Fascist.

At least, not only that.

I hopped out into the hall and leaned against the wall to catch my breath. That's when Tyler Moss sauntered by.

"Hey," he said as he passed.

"Hi," I said back. He couldn't wreck this day for me. I had just totally rocked in social studies. What does it matter that the boy you have had a crush on for months doesn't know you exist, when you have just stood with your knee in a plunger for ten minutes in front of the class and . . . Hmm.

I could feel my buzz being killed.

He looked at me, then stopped and looked again, and said, "I know you." He squinted slightly, like he was trying to decode me.

"Allison Avery. I was at Roxie Green's with you yesterday," I said, and managed not to add, *Also you hit me with your glove last February eleventh.*

He tilted his head slightly, evaluating the bit of information I'd said aloud. Clearly, he was unconvinced. "You look different."

"I wasn't holding a plunger," I said, swinging it. "And I had both legs."

He looked down and, seeing only one foot on the linoleum, opened his deep blue eyes wide with alarm.

"It's a costume," I quickly explained. "Gouverneur Morris?"

A smile broke slowly across his face, a wise-guy smile,

33

crooked and naughty. "Senator from New York?"

"No, governor," I corrected. "No! Representative!"

He laughed. "Whatever you say."

If I'd had both feet on the floor at that point I still might've wobbled, but as it was, with one foot falling asleep up near my butt, I lurched left, overcorrected, tipped right, and only managed to not fall flat on my face in front of Tyler Moss by whipping around into a drunken-looking pirouette and landing on my back.

"Interpretive dance of Mayor Morris?"

"Yeah," I answered. "Very symbolic."

"Definitely," he said, and smiled that smile again. "See, now I understand the whole Constitution."

I closed my eyes, though truly, there was little chance I would fall again, since I was still on the floor trapped like a wannabe Houdini inside my own brown corduroys. I tried to look casual by propping myself up on my elbows. "Don't you have a class first period?"

He shrugged and said, "Yeah, plumbing. But I can't find my plunger. Have you seen it?"

And then he walked away.

I MANAGED TO KEEP MY little flirt-fest to myself, luckily, because on our way out of school at the end of the day, with my Eleanor Roosevelt quote card tucked into my pocket beside my cell phone, Roxie and I rounded the corner near the gym and practically smacked right into Tyler Moss, who was leaning with his hand on the brick wall, and between him and the wall was Jade, gazing up at him and, I am not even kidding, batting her long eyelashes.

"Get a room!" Roxie called to them as we strode out the door. If they had bothered to look away from each other, they would've seen us looking totally cool and self-possessed, I am sure, despite the fact that I was crumbling inside and carrying a plunger on the outside.

"He is such a slut," Roxie said, laughing. Then she ranted as we walked out to the bus about the Fascist and how now she had to come up with a J. K. Rowling costume for tomorrow. I just agreed. The Fascist had been telling

Roxie for weeks she couldn't do Harry. I slipped into the window seat with Roxie beside me and ignored Jade, who looked especially pretty, all flushed, when she got on the bus after us.

Roxie asked loudly if I wanted to hang out at her pool again. I didn't think I could handle another afternoon of self-loathing in front of Tyler Moss, especially after watching him and Jade look so cozy, so I made up an excuse about helping Quinn with her science project to get out of going back there.

I had no idea I was sort of telling the truth.

When we got home, Gosia told us that we should stay upstairs because Mom and Dad were on their way home to have a meeting with somebody and they'd need privacy in the study. Quinn pulled me upstairs and whispered to me, in her room, "You have to get this part down there."

She thrust the baby's-room part of the baby monitor at me.

"Me?" I asked.

"You're sneakier than I am," she explained.

I couldn't argue with that. I checked the batteries—dead. Quinn yanked open an assortment of flashlights and remotes around her mess of a room until she found functional batteries that fit the monitor and the receiver. We tested it twice.

"Go!" Quinn whispered urgently.

Her face was pale, with weird little blotches of red

beside her nose and on her neck. *So much for Miss Porcelain,* I nastily thought on my way down the front staircase in my socks.

I was halfway through the silent living room when I heard a car pull up. I dashed toward the study and, sensing something nearby, straightened my back against the bookcases. Two seconds later, Gosia peeked in, plucked a microscopic piece of lint off the rug, and disappeared. My heart was thumping hard as I scouted around for a place to stash the monitor.

The desk was too obvious. The bookcase was probably too far to pick up anything.

A car door slammed. Then another.

My phone buzzed. Text from Jade:

Hey. You don't still like Ty, do u? R U mad @ me?

I cursed under my breath.

No, I texted back quickly, and kept searching for a hiding spot. On the library ladder? No way, much too conspicuous. In the trash can? I stuck it in there. Nobody would notice it. But would we hear anything? I yanked the trash can out so it sat just behind, but between, two of the chairs.

The door next to the kitchen opened. "Right through here," I heard Mom say.

I cursed again, and slapped my hand over my mouth. Then, realizing maybe Quinn would be listening, I said, whispering right into the baby monitor, "I think I'm

37

trapped. Maybe I should just hide behind the desk here."

I heard something drop upstairs and then Quinn's voice yelling, "Allison!"

I had to stop myself from laughing out loud. *Way to play it cool, Quinn.* I heard Mom offering a drink to somebody as her heels clicked across the kitchen. I had maybe three seconds.

As I dashed from the study, I realized I'd have to cross paths with Mom and whoever. I froze for half a second. Ack!

I turned and squeezed myself behind the column that held a sculpture the decorator had chosen of a hideous fat baby. The thing shimmied. If it crashed, Mom and whoever would obviously see me, cowering behind the column and among the broken pieces of overpriced clay. *Please don't fall*, I prayed, despite my atheism. The image of the devil I had dreamed flashed in my mind, and I thought, *Trade you one person thinking I'm gorgeous if you keep me invisible this once.*

The thing stopped wobbling. Probably just because it had found its equilibrium.

I'm not saying the devil interceded.

Though I did silently say a quick *Thank you* as my mother and a very tall man with a completely spherical belly preceding him walked right past me and the hideous fat baby without noticing either one of us, and turned to go into the study.

I didn't budge until after Dad followed them in, with an uncharacteristically stressed expression on his face. He closed the door behind him, and only then did I sprint silently up the front steps, contemplating my until-then-undiscovered and only gift: I could be a totally great cat burglar!

"You want to give me a heart attack?" Quinn complained.

I kissed her cheek. She hates when I do that.

What we heard was mostly static. We tried my room, which was no better. Phoebe, who wasn't around because she had track after school, got slightly better reception in her room, but the upstairs den was even better, and, following the signal, we found that the best reception was actually in one of the guest rooms behind the back stairs. We crouched over the night table, trying to hear what they were saying.

After Fat Man said ". . . legal ramifications . . . ," Quinn said, "This is what I was afraid of."

"What?"

"It's Mom's lawyer," Quinn whispered. "Those guys at work totally screwed her."

I shook my head, unsure what Quinn was talking about, but not wanting her to know that.

Fat Man asked something about a paper trail, and Mom said she would get the documents from her files. Quinn sank to the floor.

"I can't believe they screwed her like this," I said, trying to sound like I knew what I was talking about.

"I know it," Quinn agreed. "It's a team! They make the decisions on what to invest in together. They're going to make her seem like a total cowboy. She could get fired."

"Fired?" *No way,* I thought. Mom is a very successful hedge fund manager. She has been on the cover of *Working Woman* magazine. She's been in the *Wall Street Journal* and the *Columbia Business School Magazine*. She makes a ton of money. She's one of the Top Women of Wall Street. *Fired?*

"Probably not. Hopefully not. She won't." Quinn took a steadying breath and whispered, "If she gets fired, it's all over."

We heard the study door close and Mom's controlled voice saying, "Here's the time line," just as the back door opened and Phoebe came in yelling, "What's going on?"

"Get her," Quinn ordered.

I was halfway down the stairs before the thought occurred to me, *Why do I always have to do everything Quinn decides?* But instead of dealing with that, I grabbed Phoebe and dragged her noisy self up.

She is the loudest thing. She kept asking questions until I almost had to punch her in her button nose. We had trouble hearing much more, especially with Phoebe there, and then they were walking back through the kitchen, so we scooted out of the guest room and across the upstairs den to my room and shut the door so we could talk about what was happening.

Phoebe was all *You guys have to tell me*, like Quinn and I had all kinds of secret knowledge between us. I wasn't about to blow it by badgering Quinn, too, so I was just acting like I was holding back my incredibly vast knowledge of what the hell was going on instead of lacking it. In reality, I was just as anxious as Phoebe to hear Quinn's theory.

We were all sitting on my bed about to hear it when Mom and Dad opened my door and announced they were going for a ride and that our tennis instructor wasn't showing up again. Whatever.

Right after they left, Phoebe's boy-toy called on her cell phone, and she switched gears seamlessly from family-crisis mode to flirty-girl mode. Her voice got all feathery and sweet and, just like Jade, she was literally batting her eyelashes. Despite being on the freaking *phone* with the boy. *He can't see you, dim bulb!* Ugh. I almost puked all over my bed, which she and Quinn had demolished anyway with their squirming around on it.

Then on the way downstairs, Phoebe had to twist the knife by asking how it went with Tyler Moss. I explained to her as calmly as I could that Tyler Moss was an obnoxious jock whose name I never wanted to hear again. During the explanation, I may have left a permanent bruise in her flawless upper arm with my vise grip on it.

As the devil had said, alas.

And then things got really fun when at dinner Mom announced that she had been fired.

So it *was* all over, apparently.

Though exactly what was all over I had no idea, and wasn't about to ask, with Quinn, Phoebe, and Dad all silently eating their dinners. I pushed mine around and stood up as soon as Quinn did and followed her up the stairs.

"Fired," I whispered.

She closed her eyes slowly and opened them even slower.

"Like some shoplifting checkout bagger at the Food Emporium," I whispered. "Not promoted, or decided to take a job at another firm, like a normal parent. Fired."

Quinn, paler than ever, turned to me at the top of the stairs and said, "You're an idiot." Then she went to her room and closed her door softly.

Phoebe was coming up the stairs behind me, so I went into my room and closed the door, too. I taped the Eleanor Roosevelt card from Jade up on my bathroom mirror and reread it: *Do one thing every day that scares you.* I thought, *Just one thing? Is that a dare, or a limit?*

I surfed the Net for a while, then read, then just listened. Nothing going on. Was everybody really going to sleep at ten? Peeking out my door, all I saw was everybody else's closed doors, so I snuck back down the stairs to retrieve the baby monitor. *Not so stupid for an idiot, huh,* I was thinking. A big cardboard box blocked the study door. It was full of Mom's stuff: the portrait of the five of us in the silver frame, her Orrefors vase. So they'd made her clean off her desk and clear out, box of junk in hand, right in front of everybody. How humiliating.

I was just seeing what else was there when Mom suddenly sprang up behind me and screamed that I'd better get my hands off her belongings and get myself up to bed; the last thing she needed right then was trouble from me.

Great. Well, that killed my sympathy for her pretty fast.

I said some nasty stuff about her not needing to take out her work stress on me, and as much as she liked to blame me for everything, I was not the one who got her fired. She yelled back, but I wasn't listening, so I don't know which details she was highlighting about my horrible personality. A random track from *The Greatest Hits of Allison Sucks*.

I slammed my door, muttering curses under my breath. Washing up, I dimmed my bathroom light so I wouldn't have to see my hideous face.

5

Friday, Jade sat down next to me on the bus in the morning. Serena sat glumly across the aisle. "You want to come over before we go to the movies tonight?" Jade asked.

So she had forgiven me, and our movie plans were on again. I'd been thinking I'd be spending the night trolling the Internet at home, alone.

"Sure," I said.

"What should we wear?" Serena asked, leaning toward us.

Jade rolled her eyes subtly, just to me, and then said, "Just henley shirts and Hard Tails, I think. Right?"

"Yeah," I agreed. "Whatever. I'll probably wear a hoodie."

"So stylin'," Jade teased me. She pulled a pale pink lip gloss out of her bag and handed it to me. "I got an extra one for you at Sephora. My mom dragged me to the mall with her yesterday, so this was my reward. Try it."

I smoothed some across my lips, reluctantly.

Jade looked at me critically. "Nice," she said. "You definitely need gloss, Allison, or your lips disappear. And if you don't look good, I don't look good."

I tried to return her smile without losing my lips.

"So you don't like Ty anymore?" Jade whispered.

I shrugged.

"If you still do, he's dead to me."

"Thanks," I whispered back. "But, I mean, he's free to . . . Anyway, he's probably out of my . . . whatever. So go for it, if you want."

"He's probably way out of my league, too."

"I don't know about that," I said, sinking lower. "Thanks for asking, though."

"Friends first," Jade said. "Absolutely. But if you aren't putting a hold on him . . ."

"He's not a library book."

"Okay, Miss Snippy." She smiled at me, her smile that let me know I was being a bit obnoxious, but that she forgave me, all at once.

"Sorry," I muttered.

"Forget it," Jade said, bumping me with her shoulder. "And may the best girl, you know . . . not make a fool of herself over him."

"Right," I agreed.

She swiveled around in her seat toward Serena, whose sulk instantly brightened. "Doesn't Allison's hair look cute today, Serena?"

"Yes! I was just going to say—"

Jade cut her off, turning back to me. "Not frizzy at all, in the front. Do you want me to do a loose braid in the back, Allison?"

"Sure," I said. I turned away and closed my eyes while her gentle fingers tugged at my hair and then tied one of her hair bands around the bottom.

She and Serena flanked me all day long, and Roxie hardly spoke to me. That night when I got dropped off at Jade's, Serena was already there. We hung around for a while, and then Jade's dad drove us over to the mall. We wandered around until the movie started, then sank into our seats twenty minutes early, because Jade likes to get tenth row center seats and settle in without rushing. We slumped down, knees against the seats in front of us, and watched the ads and then the previews and then the movie. Afterwards, Jade's dad picked us up and drove us all home. I got dropped off first.

"Hi," Mom said when I walked in the door. She was sitting at the kitchen counter, bent over her laptop as usual. "Have fun?"

"A blast," I said, and clomped up to bed.

Another large weekend in the fabulous life of a glamour girl.

But then Saturday morning, Roxie called me. I picked up my phone from a sound sleep and it took me a minute to figure out that it wasn't Jade I was talking to. What gave it away was when she asked, "Is there anything at all to do in this town?"

"Nothing at all," I said, and sat up in my bed.

"Want to come over and watch movies all night at my house, then? Or we could play Guitar Hero, or stare at the walls until our eyes fall out?"

"Sounds awesome," I said. I took a shower, attempted to do something with my hair, gave up, and packed my bag. When I went downstairs, nobody was around, so I left a note saying where I'd be. I considered how to sign it—*Love? Love ya? Love you all?* I just wrote *Allison* and left.

The sky, finally gloomifying after weeks of gaudy blue, pressed down on everything. No birds were singing in the trees; nobody was out walking a dog or even driving too fast down our perfect street.

Hallelujah.

My phone buzzed. Jade.

Serena and I are gonna play tennis at the town courts. Want to come?

I so didn't, even though I knew Ty and those guys often hung out there, shooting hoops next to the tennis courts. I knew Jade was being generous, not wanting to sneak around and get an advantage without giving me a fair shot at equal time. *If I want any chance with Ty,* I told myself, *I should ditch Roxie and go.* The thought made me feel incredibly sleepy. I stood there holding my phone in the middle of the road.

Before I could figure out what do, Jade texted again: *What r u doing?*

I considered for a moment what to say, and then decided on something kind of bold: I told her the truth.

Going over to Roxie Green's.

In two seconds, she'd texted back

????

She's great, I answered, walking fast toward Roxie's. *We should be nice.* Jade was all about being nice, good manners, the importance of acting appropriate, so there was nothing she could say to that. I hit Send and skipped up Roxie's steps.

Absolutely. Just be careful, Jade sent back. *She's not like us. I don't trust her & I don't want u 2 b hurt.*

Thanks, I texted her. *Have fun.*

I slipped my phone into my pocket and rang Roxie's doorbell. She flung it open and said, "Great! You're here!" and pulled me in. "Do you like cookie dough?"

"Ice cream?"

"No," she said. "Just dough. I made some."

"Excellent," I said. We sank into the deepest couch I'd ever seen, surrounded by dozens of pillows, eating raw cookie dough and watching stupid stuff on TV for the rest of the afternoon. I left my phone in my bag in Roxie's front hall and didn't give it another thought. It was awesome.

At night we changed into pajamas and went to her rec house next door with flashlights. We spent about an hour jumping on her trampoline until we were sweaty and exhausted, and then we just lay there making ourselves seasick on it. Then we ran back to her regular house through the rain. We stayed up in her room until it was starting to get light out, listening to music and laughing, like when I asked her if my lips disappear when I smile. That completely cracked her up, and then me, too.

"I like the sound the rain makes against windows," she said as we were settling down to sleep under puffy comforters.

"I'm just glad the weather has finally caught up with my personality," I said.

We fell asleep giggling and didn't wake up until noon.

Over bowls of cereal on that dreary Sunday afternoon, Roxie's mother, Jenny, brought up the idea that changed everything.

"There's an open call tomorrow," she said from behind a newspaper called *Backstage*.

"Modeling?" Roxie asked.

"Yes," Jenny answered. "Hey, Allison, you know *zip*?"

"Yeah," I said, feeling myself blush. "Approximately." What had I done that was so stupid?

Roxie, laughing, went and found a copy of a magazine called *zip* in a basket near their back door. I recognized it as the same one I had taken from Phoebe's room the other night, but I just shrugged. I hate those magazines—all those skinny, perfect girls selling junk.

Jenny shoved over the ten boxes of cereal she had taken out for us to choose among and laid down the paper. Her smile and dimples were as bright and cute as Roxie's, though her voice was deeper and more ragged.

She pushed her long, wavy hair back from her forehead with her thumb and pinky and read the ad out loud to us:

" '*Zip* magazine, looking for edgy but clean-cut nonpros for feature on the new teen. All types, open call. Monday, May nineteenth, ten a.m. to one p.m.'

"Then the address and all that. What do you say?" Jenny looked at us, full of gung-ho enthusiasm. "You two are definitely edgy but clean-cut!"

"We are?" Roxie asked dubiously.

"Compared to how I was at your age, hell, yeah," Jenny said, and laughed. She propped her knees up on the table and shook her head. "At least clean-cut. And edgy is easy: all in the clothes."

"Modeling?" I said. "Not me, obviously."

"But you're exactly the type," Jenny said. She leaned forward to get a closer look.

I ducked my head and said, "I'm not."

"Oh, come on, Allison," Roxie begged. "You're my right-handed man. Let's just go. Gotta be better than school, right?"

"Well, if it's okay with your mom," Jenny offered, getting up to put away the cereal boxes, "I can drive you girls to the train tomorrow morning."

"I'll ask," I lied.

Roxie and I went back up to her room, and over the course of the day, I gave in little by little. I didn't put up that much of a fight, if I'm honest. I gave in when she said I could just go and hang out with her. I didn't have to get my picture taken at all if I didn't want to, and anyway, wouldn't it be better than being at school?

Honestly, there was no possible argument against that.

But I knew there was no way my parents would ever let me cut school to go with Roxie Green to have her picture taken. No matter how much my parents say it's important to stand by your friends, they don't completely mean it. Like, Mom and Jade's mom only smile tightly when they see each other now. They used to sit on a park bench and totally gossip all summer when we were little. So I knew I'd never win that argument on the merits. Anyway, they had been saying for my whole life that I should be less argumentative.

That's why I decided not to have the argument.

Also, they were having enough arguments without me. Since I hadn't gotten the baby monitor out of the study, I listened in when they were whispering at each other Sunday night. I couldn't hear the whole thing, but it was definitely about money. Mom was saying, "I've got it under control, Jed," and "We really don't need the entire neighborhood buzzing about our business"; he kept murmuring to her, too, lots that I couldn't hear, but what I did hear him say was, "I just think it's inappropriate to be spending that kind of money right now on a party for an eighth-grade graduation. It's obscene! And we can't, Claire. We can't."

"Don't say we can't," she snarled. "I can certainly—"

"She's canceling," he said. "It's done."

Then they were back to whispering, but that was enough. Obviously they were making Phoebe cancel her graduation party, poor thing. I wondered how Phoebe would deal.

Knowing her, she would just somehow turn it to her advantage and become even more popular.

Roxie texted me as I was drifting off to sleep that night that she had told her mother I had to drop off something first period and then they could pick me up at the corner down from school to go to the train. I texted back

OK, then placed my phone beside the baby monitor on my nightstand and stared at both things without blinking until my eyes burned.

I went to sleep to the lullaby of my parents' whispered arguments, and woke up before dawn, dreading the day.

6

I GUESS I WAS KIND OF a wreck in the morning waiting for the bus, because Quinn asked what was wrong with me in a way that made me think she somehow knew what I was planning to do. I swore her to secrecy and told her.

"You're cutting school?"

"Just this once," I explained.

"Why? Perversity?"

"Maybe," I said. "If I knew what that word meant, I would tell you if that's the reason."

Quinn rolled her eyes. "It's like, being bad just for the sake of being bad."

"Oh," I said. "No. Not perversity. Being bad just for the sake of being a good friend. Per*friend*ity."

She shook her head, disappointed. "Since when are you even friends with Roxie Green? Who cuts school to wander around the city and get her picture taken by God knows who? I don't think I like this girl."

"Well, you don't have to," I said.

"Think, Allison. You're taking a train and then a subway to God knows where without permission so some stranger can take pictures of you?"

"Roxie knows where, too," I insisted. "She's from there. Don't worry."

Quinn opened her light blue eyes very wide. "Are you an idiot or suicidal?"

"Neither," I said. "And I'm not getting MY picture taken, I told you. I'm just going with Roxie. I'll be back at school before the end of the day, so nobody will— You know what? Forget it. I shouldn't have told you—"

"You're an idiot," she interrupted me. "Just what Mom and Dad need right now is trouble from you again."

"Don't tell them," I warned her. "You promised."

"I won't! I have no intention of hurting them. But can't you just— Fine, whatever. Have fun." She climbed up onto the bus ahead of me.

"Thanks," I said to her back, just as sarcastically.

I sat with my knee bopping uncontrollably through first period, where I got a slip of paper at the end of the class with the Fascist's crinkled purple writing on it:

Excellent presentation. Thought-provoking. A–.

I crumpled it in my hand as I left the classroom and shoved it into my backpack. A–? Fine, whatever. I headed toward the back door and, rounding a corner, almost slammed into Ms. Chen, the principal, who said, "Let's see some smiles, students! Learning is exhilarating!"

I managed a smile for her, like, *Excellent pep talk; my life is turned around now*, before I hurried down the stairs and out of there. Roxie and her mom were in the car at the bottom of the hill with the motor running and the radio on full blast. I slipped into the backseat and slumped down to make my getaway.

"You're bringing your backpack?"

I thought of making up an excuse, but couldn't come up with one. "I never go to my locker," I admitted. "I'm not even sure where it is, maybe over by the gym somewhere? I don't know. Anyway, I kind of forgot the combination by now."

Roxie's mom cracked up, the same loud, barky laugh as Roxie. It was the kind of laugh that was hard to resist joining in on. "That is excellent," she said as we pulled into the train station. "Lost your locker. I love it. Have fun!"

As she drove away, I said to Roxie, "Your mom has the coolest voice. Like almost smoky."

"She used to be a DJ, before she had me."

"You can totally hear why," I said. "A DJ. That's so cool."

"What about your mom?" Roxie asked, looking down the tracks for the train. "What's she like? Typical suburban mom?"

"No. She's a hedge fund manager," I said, and when

Roxie looked blank about that, I explained, "It's, like, with money. She's the smartest person I've ever met, the most beautiful, the most perfect."

"Wow," Roxie said. "That must suck."

I laughed, feeling a wave of surprising relief flood through me. "It does," I said as the train thundered into the station. "Nobody ever got that before. Including me, I think."

Roxie shrugged. "My mother used to be a total hellion."

"Really?" I asked. "She seems so sweet."

"Well, she nods too much, like my dad," Roxie said. "But yeah, she's pretty sweet."

"I bet my mom would like her," I said, and then shrugged because maybe that sounded like my mother was desperate for friends or something. Sometimes I could just slap myself.

As we settled into a two-seat, I noticed that Roxie had a manila envelope in her hand. I asked her what it was, so she handed it to me. In the envelope were three identical pictures of Roxie. I pulled one out. In it, she was even prettier than in real life, her freckles gone and her eyes more sparkly than usual, her head ducked slightly enough to make her look simultaneously innocent and sexy.

"Wow," I said, turning it over to read her stats and résumé.

"It's from last year," Roxie said casually. "Doesn't look

like I'll end up tall enough to do runway or anything, but maybe I can keep doing commercials and catalogues."

"Uh-huh," I said. We just sat there not talking the rest of the ride in. *A model,* I was thinking. And ugly-duckling me. What a joke we must look like. Why hadn't I thought of putting on at least some of the makeup Jade had given me over the past year? If Jade thought I was mildly unattractive, what must a legitimate model think? I sank down low in my chair for a private little self-hate-fest.

"What do you think of Emmett O'Leary?" Roxie asked as we got swept up in the crowd getting off the train.

I made a slightly nauseated face at the thought that maybe she somehow knew I'd totally crushed on Emmett O'Leary when I was in seventh grade, and asked why.

"Nothing," she said, pulling me to the left and down a big flight of stairs. "Seems like a nice guy. Kind of sweet."

"I guess," I said, unsure if she was trying to fix me up with him because I had no shot at Tyler. Not wanting to seem too anything, I added the only criticism I could come up with of Emmett: "Pale."

"Yeah, but who cares?" She whipped a thin plastic card out of her wallet and skimmed it through a reader. "Go," she told me, so I went through a turnstile ahead of her, squished together so it only made one turn.

A subway train roared by on a middle track. I stuck my fingers in my ears when Roxie did, and thought how babyish and followerish I must seem to her. *Ugh,* I thought. *I have become Serena! Somebody shoot me now!*

Just kidding, I added silently, not looking at the two scary guys to my left.

We smooshed onto a packed subway car and jostled our way to the middle of the crowd on the train. I had no idea where I was or how to get home from there. *Quinn was right,* I admitted to myself as a huge woman whapped me with one of her six bags. I was an absolute idiot.

"This is us," Roxie said after a few stops. I followed her off the train, up a steep set of stairs that smelled like pee. As she practically jogged along the street and I hustled to keep up, I checked my cell phone, considering calling home and asking someone to come pick me up. I knew I wouldn't, though. I'd just end up in trouble if I did. Meanwhile, Roxie was stalking down the block and into a line of tall, beautiful girls stretching down the block outside a squat brick building.

She spread on lip gloss and leaned against the bricks. I hid behind my hair. I checked my cell phone again. It was still being completely normal and silent. Not even a text from Jade asking where I was.

We waited some more. Roxie checked her hair and smile in a mirror from her bag. I checked my watch.

"Do you like the Black Eyed Peas?"

I shrugged, not sure what black-eyed peas were, exactly. "Do you?"

"Sure," she said. "I like all bands with colors in their

names. Black Eyed Peas, Plain White T's . . ."

"Green Day," I added, and when she smiled, I was relieved. I'm actually pretty out of it, music-wise, and kind of pulled that name out of nowhere—I was scared for a sec it wasn't even the name of a band.

"Exactly," she said. "That's what I like about you, Al. You totally get it."

She couldn't have been more wrong, but I wasn't about to correct her on that. I wasn't who she thought I was. I was even more nobody than usual, because I was also nowhere. At least, nobody knew where I was. Nobody knew who I was. Like so many great poets, I was anonymous. Maybe I could be a poet, I decided. Too bad I can't write poetry.

After about an hour, we got through the door and up to the desk, where a skinny guy with spiky peroxide hair and dark-rimmed glasses sat at a desk in front of the sign-in book at 12:12. Roxie bent down to sign her name.

The guy pointed behind him, so Roxie and I started heading toward the line of bored-looking girls waiting there.

"You have to sign in," he said to me.

"I'm not really here," I explained.

"My mistake," he said. "Where are you, then, in school?"

I smiled. "Yeah, fourth period." Then I started around his little desk toward Roxie.

He grabbed my wrist and said, "You want to be seen,

60

you have to sign in."

"But I don't want to be seen."

"Well, then, you forgot to sprinkle on your fairy dust this morning, darlin', because I see you."

"Even though I didn't sign in?"

He took a weary sip of his coffee. "Don't be a pain in my ass, huh, dear? Sign in or leave."

"Come on," Roxie yelled. A very tall, gaunt woman was holding open an elevator door and beckoning the girls.

I bent down and scribbled my name, leaving out one of my L's—*Alison Avery*, I wrote. To be more anonymous. Or less me, less there.

"Phone number?" the guy said. "Preferably cell."

I smiled to myself and, as I was writing down my number, muttered, "My cell phone is possessed by the devil."

"Aren't they all?" he answered.

I smiled up at him and then dashed across the concrete space toward Roxie. The elevator door closed behind me and up we went.

7

FOR ONCE IN MY LIFE I was one of the shortest girls in the room. These girls were practically giraffes. We could've taken on the Knicks. If anybody needed a can of stewed tomatoes from a top shelf, we were totally on the job.

And there might have been three percent body fat in the room, on average. Not that I was obese, but you know how they say if Bill Gates walked into a room of a thousand homeless people, the average net worth in the room would shoot up to millions per person? Yeah, well, I was like the Bill Gates of body fat in that room.

The widest part of the girl's legs on the metal chair beside me was her knees. It was seriously alarming.

Nobody talked or smiled. We all just sat there gorgeously wasting away, except for me. I just sat there.

One by one our names were called. Knees Girl was right before Roxie, so when she went to door number two, Roxie held my hand. Hers was clammy. I squeezed it. When a bored-looking guy with a British accent called her name, she crossed her eyes at me and strutted across the room. I had to smile. She was way prettier than any of those other skeletons. But I did notice, as she crossed the room away from me, that she was really skinny, too.

My phone started playing unrecognizable jazz. I was grabbing it out of my pocket when Mr. British Empire frowned like something smelled rancid and said, "No cell phones."

"I'm not . . ." Just as I got it out, it died completely.

"That's better," he said. The door to room three opened and he sighed, saying, "Alison Avery."

I stood up to explain my situation as a six-foot-tall girl ambled out of the room, biting her puffy pink lip and holding a sultry, much more attractive picture of herself in her long fingers.

"Go in, phone girl," English Accent Guy said. "Go in, unless we're interrupting you."

I leaned toward him and tried to explain quietly, "No, I just . . . I'm not—"

"I don't care, go!"

Feeling all the beautiful eyes in the room on me, I went.

"Stand on the line," a woman with a pale blond bob ordered as the door slammed behind me.

I stood on the blue line of tape and said, "I'm not really—"

"No talking."

She raised a Polaroid camera and aimed it at me as if it were a gun. I normally hate having my picture taken, but I had to almost laugh at the thought that I'd somehow been tried and sentenced to death by firing squad for the offense of cutting school.

The flash practically blinded me. The Camera Nazi took two steps back and said, "Stop blinking. Jacket off."

"I don't really . . . Fine, whatever." I dropped my zip-up sweatshirt on the floor and stood there in my tank top feeling like a total dork while she snapped another picture.

"Allison Avery," she said, writing my name on the margins of the two photos as I bent down to retrieve my sweatshirt. "Oh. Only one L in Alison?"

"I lost one on the way in," I said, heading for the door.

"Interesting-looking," she said.

"So they say," I muttered with my hand on the door handle.

"Wait," Blondie ordered.

I turned around.

She came close and stared at me like she was looking at a picture, with no expectation that I was there and alive, looking back. It felt beyond weird. "Yes," she said. "Interesting. We'll see. Go."

Roxie was waiting for me near the big metal door near the elevator, with a smile pressing her dimples deep into her face. "How'd you do?"

"Well, they didn't fingerprint me," I said. "You?"

She laughed and threw her arm around my shoulders. "Thanks for coming with me. You're the first normal person I've met since moving out to the burbs."

It was the first time anybody'd accused me of being normal.

In the elevator going down, she whispered to me, "I have to tell you something, but not here."

I nodded and stayed as silent as the three other stick figures in there with us and a completely bald guy in a purple blouse.

Out on the street, Roxie linked her elbow through mine and started walking fast. I had to take huge steps to keep up with her. "My mom is picking us up at the two-forty-seven, so we have time. That was quicker than I thought, but you will never believe what happened!"

"What?" I asked her. For once the sun wasn't offending me. People were jostling by us with scowls on their faces, talking psychotically to nobody but—at least I had to figure in most cases—their hidden cell phone ear things. Women in heels I'd never manage just standing still in were beating men in wingtips in dead sprints across packed intersections, as cabs beeped and buses groaned.

Two little white dogs turned up their noses as they passed each other in the crosswalk, and a four-foot-tall woman with hot-pink hair decorated in bits of tinfoil barked curses at nobody in particular.

It was great.

"Okay," Roxie finally said, leading me into a Star-bucks.

"What happened?" I asked her as we waited in line.

She grinned. "They took two."

"Two what?"

"Two pictures," she whispered. "Usually they just take the close-up, but the guy who looked at me was all, like, 'Oh, yeah, good,' and then he said he wanted to get a three-quarter view, so he took that, too!"

"That's great," I said, not wanting to disappoint her by letting her know they wasted a second picture on me, too, so that was probably standard. "Seriously, Roxie."

She scrunched up her nose. "I think so, too." We had reached the front of the line, so she turned to the barista and said, "Hi how are you I'd like a half-caf tall sugar-free vanilla skim extra-hot latte, please. Al?"

I was just going to get a water like usual, but her order sounded so sophisticated. I didn't want to seem like a sub-urban baby, but I also didn't want to be like Serena the Shadow and just order whatever she had, so I ordered what my mom usually gets. She worked in the city. Or she had until she got fired.

"Doppio macchiato, please."

Roxie looked at me with big open eyes and said, "Wow," so I figured I'd ordered well.

We paid, which used up most of the money in my wallet, picked up our drinks, and took them out into the bright sunshine again. Two steps down the sidewalk Roxie stopped short at a sunglass table and we tried on a few pairs for each other while sipping our drinks. Mine was seriously hot and the most vile, bitter thing I'd ever tasted, but I didn't want to be like, *Ew! What the heck is this, engine grease?* So I just tried to swallow tiny sips without letting it touch my tongue, in between modeling sunglasses.

As we tried them on, Roxie told me this story about how she and a friend of hers (her old right-handed man) from the city went one time last year to the makeup counter at Bloomingdale's and Roxie said she thought she had left her sunglasses there while trying on makeup a few days earlier. The lady asked what color and Roxie said sort of brownish? And the lady hauled this big plastic bin up onto the counter and let Roxie try on all the lost sunglasses until she'd found a pair she liked.

"Where's Bloomingdale's?" I asked.

Roxie grinned. "You are so bad." She looked at her watch. "We don't have time."

That's not even what I meant, but she looked so delighted with me I didn't say, *No, I was just making conversation and trying to avoid jealous questions about this old right-handed man who seemed so much more fun and wilder than me.* Roxie had a pair of red sunglasses on, so I grabbed another pair just like them so we could smoosh our heads together in the mirror and make faces. We actually looked pretty cool, I have to say, and Roxie insisted they were the bomb on me, so she bought them for me as a thank-you present for coming with her. I told her she didn't have to, but she insisted and then bought the matching pair for herself and we walked on, linked again but now shaded, with coffee drinks.

"*We* are the bomb," I said, and she threw her head back and laughed out loud.

As we crossed a huge street the light changed, so we decided to just hang on the bench there on the island between lanes of traffic.

"If I tell you something," Roxie said, looking straight ahead, her legs stretched out ahead of her, "will you promise never to tell anyone?"

"I told you the other day," I reminded her, "I am like the Fort Knox of secrets. I never reveal anything. It's my only virtue."

"Really?"

"Sad but true." I said. "Who would I tell, anyway? You're pretty much the only person in school still talking to me."

"Your best friend is kind of a prig."

"Yeah," I said, feeling shaky though not really nervous. Why would I be nervous? "She's great, but opinionated."

"If you say so," Roxie said doubtfully. "Seems to me like the cheese has blown completely off her cracker."

I laughed. "You think?"

"No doubt," Roxie said seriously. "So, swear you won't tell, even her?"

"I swear I won't tell Jade or anybody else what you are about to tell me," I said. My heart was pounding hard, though I totally didn't feel worried about keeping her secret. I'm not good at much, but I really can keep a secret.

"We didn't move to the suburbs because of gardening."

"Okay," I said. Sweat was starting to soak my forehead.

"We moved because of me," she whispered, leaning back to look at the sky.

I took another sip of the crude oil in my cup and tried to calm myself down. What was going on with me?

"I didn't get into high school," she whispered.

"What do you mean?" I took off my sweatshirt jacket and sat there sweating and shaking like a junkie in my tank top. Luckily Roxie was staring at the sky, so she didn't notice.

She smiled, but not her normal happy smile—a tight, sad smile. "Private school, right? I went to a K-through-eight, so in eighth grade you have to apply out. I was, like, whatever, not stressed, you know? I mean, my parents know everybody and obviously I wasn't going to Brearley or whatever, but . . ."

She kept talking about schools I had never heard of

as if anybody would know why you would roll your eyes about one place or another. I was busy trying not to have a heart attack in the middle of traffic. *Deep breaths,* I was telling myself, catching just bits and pieces of what she was saying, until the punch line. "Zero for eight. Not even wait-listed, and my mother is on the board there."

"That sucks."

"To put it mildly," she said. "My parents are all, like, 'It was just bad luck. Or a tough year.' A lot of the schools are like eenie-meenie-miney-moe, my mom says, and apparently I just was never moe."

"Eh," I said. "Who'd want to be moe, anyway? Moe blows."

She smiled a little. "Or maybe I'm just stupid."

"You are so not stupid!" I swabbed my face with my sweatshirt.

"Yeah, well, my former right-handed man was telling me about her cousin who got rejected from everywhere, and that everybody was all, 'It was a tough year,' but in truth it's just that the cousin was kind of dim."

"Your former right-handed man has no cheese on her cracker." I put my half-full cup down on the pavement with my shaking hands while Roxie chuckled. "Or whatever you said before. Your parents are completely right. You are so obviously smart it's ridiculous."

"I guess it's just easier to believe the bad stuff," Roxie said.

"Yeah, well," I started, knowing exactly how she felt. "Maybe you just have to get over that."

Roxie looked up at the sky. "Easy to say."

I accidentally kicked over my cup with my jiggling foot and said, "I think there's a lot of caffeine in this."

Roxie cracked up and said, "You think?" She grabbed the empty cup and tossed it into the wire trash can beside us. "Doppio macchiato!"

"Yeah," I said. "I actually have no idea what it is."

She laughed loud and hard. "It's a double shot of espresso!"

"Yeah, well, it tastes like crude oil."

"Forget Alison with one L," Roxie said, wiping tears from her eyes but still laughing. "From now on, I call you Double Shot."

"If I die of a heart attack here, don't tell my mother I got my picture taken, okay?"

She looked at me, full of concern. "You look like hell."

"Thanks," I said.

She helped me up and we walked awhile. I started feeling better after maybe five blocks, but I kept my arm around her shoulder for a few more anyway. When we got to Grand Central Terminal, we were still ten minutes early, so we sat on the sidewalk leaning against each other.

"Thanks," Roxie said.

"For practically passing out?"

"No," she said. "For not being all, 'You are so dumb no high school wanted you, you loser.'"

"It was easy. I don't think that." I shrugged. "Anyway, I'm glad you moved, even if you're not. What would I be doing if you'd gotten into one of those stupid private schools?"

"Not having heart palpitations on the sidewalk?" she offered. "Hanging out with Jade and Hyena?"

"Serena."

"Whatever."

"Yeah," I agreed. "So, lucky for me you weren't moe."

She smiled at me, that radiant smile that got her into all those toy catalogues and pajama ads. "You could totally do commercials," she said.

"Could not," I said, and then put on a fake smile and said, all cheery, "I just love fast food!" Then I laughed. "No way."

"Don't mock," she said. "You have a cool look."

"Ugh."

"Seriously," she said. "You, my friend, are cooler than the other side of the pillow."

That cracked me up until she started looking at me the way the woman at the photo shoot had, like I wasn't inside my own skin. "You have a really cool look, plus, you're gorgeous."

"Well, if I am, it cost me my cell phone."

"What did?"

"Nothing," I said.

"Come on," she said, leaning close and searching my eyes. "What cost you what?"

I sighed. "I sold my cell phone to the devil and in exchange, seven—well, maybe six—people will think I'm gorgeous. So if you think I'm gorgeous, that only leaves me five more people."

"Holy crap," she said. "You know the devil! Really?"

"Obviously not really. That's the dream I had the other night. Weird, right? The devil was in my bedroom. Wonder what my ex-shrink would say about that!"

"So was it real or a dream, then?"

"Come on, Roxie," I said, feeling like an idiot for not realizing she'd obviously been teasing me.

"What?" she asked, all innocent and big-eyed.

"You don't actually believe in the devil and neither do I. Obviously."

"I don't know," she said with great seriousness, turning to face me. "My father believes in God, my mother believes in me, the Fascist believes I actually read all seven Harry Potter books, and everybody I know in this city believes I got into Dalton but that my parents had a midlife crisis that involved peat moss and sod. So who's got a lock on what's real?"

I wasn't sure what to think about all that, so I just said, "Okay."

She shrugged, agreeing, and then asked, "Doesn't the

devil usually make deals for your soul?"

"I don't have one, apparently."

"Awesome," Roxie said. "Think he'd want my cell phone too?"

I laughed. "If he shows up again, I'll ask."

"Thanks!" She looked genuinely excited, her bright blue eyes all sparkly. "But about me not getting in anywhere . . ."

"I will never tell anyone your secrets, Roxie."

She smiled, until her cell phone rang. She grabbed it, cursed, and picked up. "No!" she said into it, jumping up and dashing toward the door. "We're at Grand Central, but . . ."

I looked up the clock. It was 2:53.

"Okay. Yup, yup," she said, zigzagging through the crowds. "Track seventeen. We'll be on it. Okay. Sorry, Mom!"

When she flipped her phone closed she shook her head and said, "See what I mean? Total airhead, and she still believes in me. Nuts, right?"

"That must be weird," I said, and surprised myself when my voice cracked.

Luckily Roxie didn't seem to notice.

We slumped against each other the whole way home, listening to Roxie's iPod with one earbud each. Jenny dropped me at the curb, and I walked up the driveway feeling more okay than usual, despite the fact that I'd ingested more caffeine than in the rest of my life combined and also that I had just cut school and gone into the city without permission. Normally, any of those things would have me jumping out of my skin. Instead I was practically humming.

Then I saw that Mom's car was already in our driveway.

I stood there paralyzed for a few seconds, feeling the best day of my year drain away fast. *I am so busted,* I told myself.

Think!

Think like the cat burglar you are.

There was a trellis leading up the side of the house, covered in rose vines but still climbable. I dropped my backpack in the bushes and headed toward it, hoping I wouldn't fall off the roof at the top before Quinn could let me in through her window.

$\mathcal{8}$

BANGING ON QUINN'S window unbalanced me, and I thought for a moment there that I was about to fall off the roof and splat to my death on the front walk. As I teetered, I had time to wonder if Tyler Moss would come to my funeral, and if Jade would give a speech talking about the depth of our friendship.

I clutched onto the shutter until Quinn whipped open the window and yanked me into her room, criticizing me in her whispery voice before my feet even hit the red rug.

I tried to explain to her that we'd missed the train, but she was interrupting me all over the place, and then I noticed that Phoebe, of all people, was standing there staring at me.

"What are you doing here?" I asked her, really accusing Quinn, though. Leave it to Quinn to go blabbing about me when I confide in her, I was thinking. When I never would tell any of her secrets, especially not to Phoebe, who obviously knew something, because right away she asked if I'd cut school.

Fine, I decided. *Screw it.* So I told her where I'd gone. She was shocked, which was kind of adorable, especially when she asked me why we'd gone into the city all by ourselves, like we were ducklings or something.

I told her we had gone to become fashion models.

Her face was priceless. Trying so hard not to betray the fact that she knew there was no way I could ever be anything of the kind, Phoebe puzzled that for a few seconds before rearranging her lovely features into a radiant smile and saying, "No, but really. Why did you go into the city?"

I had to laugh. She was right not to believe it. The devil in my bedroom was a more plausible occurrence than me trying to be a fashion model. "Yeah, thanks," I said, and, when she looked sorry and about to correct my (actually correct) impression of her disbelief, continued, "Ugh. Don't even ask. You try to do a friend a favor and you end up getting your picture taken by a bunch of creeps with fake English . . ."

I didn't get to finish because Quinn was freaking out that I'd gotten my picture taken. Like it mattered anyway. To change the subject I asked what they were doing.

It turned out Phoebe hadn't canceled her graduation party after all, and the invitations to it had just come in the mail. And even worse, Mom's check for the deposit had bounced, so our financial situation was about to become the talk of the town.

Poor Phoebe was practically shaking.

And Quinn, the tightass, was just making her feel worse.

I told Phoebe I'd help her get money, and she looked so grateful I couldn't help hugging her. Poor thing, she had no idea how to handle friendship stress or any kind of stress—everything had always fallen into place for her. *Must be nice to be the baby of the family,* I thought. I was the baby for just over a year but didn't know enough as an infant to take full advantage of the situation.

Surprisingly my generous offer didn't perk Phoebe right up; she started to do that trembling-lip thing she does when she cries that could just break your heart (if you had one; mine, I figured, was probably on vacation in Tahiti with my soul; but still, even I felt a little bad for her).

The three of us all scooted into Quinn's gigantic closet and sat on her chaotic mess of stuff. I tried not to look around too much. How can a person who is so perfect in every other way be such a slob? Little by little Phoebe coughed up the rest of the story—her friends, basically, were dumping her.

I promised Phoebe we'd come up with the money she needed for her party, but Quinn was all like, *No way, you can't, Mommy and Daddy will never let you,* blah blah blah. She was totally destroying Phoebe, right there in the closet, breaking her into little bits. I couldn't believe it. Usually I was the nasty one.

Of course, Phoebe just lumped me right in there with Quinn's meanness despite my (probably creaky from disuse) sweet generosity, and stomped out of the closet, out of Quinn's room, cursing and slamming doors behind her as she went.

I turned to Quinn to ask her why she was being so awful to Phoebe, but got a dose of it for myself before I had a chance.

"Grow up," Quinn spat at me. "You have to get your head out of your ass, Allison. This family is falling apart and what are you doing? Cutting school, climbing onto the roof, convincing Phoebe you can . . . what? Rob a bank for her?"

"Rob? My own account, you jerk," I said. "I wasn't offering *your* money, you tightass."

I managed to get up off her war zone of a closet floor and out into her room. "You can pretend you're a martyr all you want," I said, heading toward her door. "Is it really helping anybody? Is it getting Mom her job back? And thanks for showing me I can really count on you to keep my secrets. Not."

I opened her door and slammed it shut behind me before I saw that Mom was standing there in the upstairs hall staring at me.

"Hi," I said, trying to smile.

She stared at me for a few more seconds as curses and strategies chased each other through my brain. How much had she heard? Did she know I hadn't come in through the front door? What should I say if she confronts me on whether I cut school? Cutting was bad, but lying about it would be way worse, unless I didn't get caught, so . . .

"Everything okay?" she asked me.

My heart was slamming against my ribs again. "Um, yeah," I said. "You?"

She let out a sigh/laugh. "I've had better weeks, actually."

She took a sip from the mug in her hand, and glanced at the papers in the other.

I was scared to move a muscle, so I just stood there and said, "Mmm."

Then my phone rang and vibrated in my pocket. As I was grabbing it, she turned away, but then turned back and said, "Did you know everything you text on a cell phone is recoverable?"

"Um," I said. The call was coming from a number I didn't recognize. I didn't know whether to answer or not.

"So be careful," Mom said, and drifted away, sipping her coffee.

"I will," I said to her back, and flipped open my phone.

"Allison Avery," said an unfamiliar voice.

"Yes?"

"This is Natasha Mendel."

"Okay," I said.

"From *zip*."

My first thought was that I must have left my backpack there, but no, it was down in the bushes, which reminded me I should go get it after I hung up, despite the fact that, since I cut, I wouldn't know what the homework was anyway. As I was thinking all that, I was walking across the hall to my own room but not saying anything.

"Hello?" the voice said.

"Yes," I said, and sat down on my little beige couch, my favorite thing in my thankfully neat, clean room in shades of beige and white that Jade had helped me pick out. Jade's mom had said neutrals are calming, and Jade pointed out the obvious, that I needed all the help with achieving calm I could get.

My call waiting clicked. I looked and, weirdly, it was Jade. Had she sensed me thinking about her?

I was about to ask the woman from *zip* to hold on, but then I remembered how freaky my cell phone had been acting and, out of fear I'd lose her, decided I'd call Jade back later, and realized the woman from the magazine was asking me in kind of a snotty, annoyed voice if she was calling at a bad time.

"No," I told her. "This is fine."

"You didn't drop off a picture today," said Ms. Natasha Mendel.

"I didn't know you had to," I said.

"You didn't," she said. "We were just wondering if you have management."

"Um," I said, because I didn't know what that meant.

"Is there an agent or manager we need to speak with?"

"About what?"

"About you," Natasha Mendel said.

"What did I do?"

"You photographed strikingly," she said.

I sank down onto the floor. "Strikingly?"

"You are among our twenty semifinalists," she said.

"You've got to be kidding," I said, and then realized what it must be. "Who is this? Roxie? Is that you?"

"Who?"

"Come on, Roxie, I know it's you," I said, pacing around my room. "You had me there for a second, I admit it, but I know your voice, you stinker!"

"How old are you?" she asked.

"Fifteen, same as you! Enough already, seriously, Roxie. Are you three-way calling me?" I was starting to sweat again. If there is one thing I hate, it's getting punked on the phone.

"I am far from fifteen," the voice said. "We will be mailing you some parental consent forms to move forward with the next step, and I require your address, Allison. I have no time for adolescent behavior."

I didn't say anything. I was too confused.

"Your address?" the voice, which actually didn't sound remotely like Roxie's, repeated.

Knowing I was never allowed to give out my address to a stranger over the phone or the computer, I listened with some surprise to myself reciting my address.

"Return the forms promptly," she said when I finished. "And meanwhile, I have you down as unrepresented. It will be best for you if you keep that status. We are looking to discover new talent in this competition."

"Okay," I said, and hung up not knowing really what had just happened, or what to believe.

9

I CALLED ROXIE FIRST. While her phone was ringing, I talked myself down. It was probably a prank, and if it wasn't, if somehow a person from *zip* had actually called me, I must have misunderstood—like maybe there was a fee for getting my picture taken that I hadn't realized I was supposed to pay or something.

"Hey," Roxie said, picking up. "How's it going, Double Shot?"

"Um, fine," I said.

"You're not in trouble, are you?"

"Um, no," I said equally eloquently. My legs were shaking as I paced fast around the room, waiting for her to shriek that she had just gotten a callback from *zip*. If she did, should I tell her I had, too?

"You okay?" she asked. "You sound stressed. Still hyper-caffed?"

"No, no," I told her. "Well, maybe. Yeah. But . . . I

84

was . . . It's the weirdest—you didn't just call me, did you?"

"No, I was just peeing. Why? Oh! Is your phone freaking out? Maybe it's the devil!"

"Probably," I said. "There wasn't a . . . We didn't . . ."

"Spit it out, Double Shot!"

"I just was thinking," I said. "When do you think we, or you, might hear from the, you know, people at the magazine?"

"Within the week," she said. "They move fast. If we don't hear anything by Thursday night, we're out. Hey, wouldn't it be so awesome if we both got into the running?"

"Yeah, wow, that would be, but . . ."

"I know, I know you're not into it, but trust me, it's so fun getting your picture taken for stuff like that. I've never done editorial, but even a catalogue—I mean, there's a lot of boring time, just sitting around, but you have all these people putting on your makeup and doing your hair and dressing you in wacky clothes, and the photographers are all like, 'Oh, you are so gorgeous'—well, most of them anyway—but trust me, it's great."

"I think I'd throw up," I said, feeling exactly that way already.

"Oh, look down your nose at the whole thing, you're probably right. It's not curing cancer. But the girl who got the cover in the teen issue last year has her own TV show starting next fall."

"Really?"

"Not even kidding. Anyway, the odds are never good on something like this, I know. You almost never get to be moe, right? My mom says all the time you just have to keep a good attitude, but anyway just cross your fingers for me, okay? I could use a win."

I crossed my fingers, closed my eyes, and said, "Okay."

"You want to come swim or watch a movie or something?"

"No, I should deal," I mumbled.

"Okay. Call me later," she said, and hung up.

I stared at my phone for a few minutes, daring the devil to call me to check in. He didn't, so I called Jade back.

"Hello, Allison," she said in her deep, raspy voice.

"Hello, Jade," I said.

Then I waited.

"You weren't in school after first today," Jade said.

"No," I said, and nothing more, knowing that if I rushed her, Jade would just hang up on me and the whole episode would be needlessly extended. She was angry— obviously—again.

"Are you sick?"

"No," I said.

"So you cut?"

"Yeah," I said.

"With Roxanne Green?"

"Yup," I said. I was being more of a jerk than usual with her, and I knew it. I wasn't sure why. I guess I just wasn't in the mood.

"What did you and Roxanne Green do?" She kept saying *Roxanne Green* as if it were the name of a bacterium.

"We went into the city and became supermodels, and then we took drugs and prostituted ourselves. Then we had a coffee and came home."

She didn't respond.

"Kidding," I said. "We didn't take drugs."

"Listen, Allison. You can be sarcastic all you want, but you should know that your friends are worried about you."

"Worried?" I sat down on my couch, feeling the energy drain from my legs.

"It's just not like you," Jade said softly, her voice more confidential than condemning. "Cutting school? Assaulting a teacher? Hanging out with Roxanne Green? Acting all slutty?"

"What are you talking about, slutty? Me?" It had to be a joke. I'd never even come close to kissing a boy, or even flirting with one, unless you count getting hit by a mitten, or falling on my butt. Which you really can't. The only thing was, Jade didn't joke. Especially not about sluttiness.

"The way you've been strutting around lately," she said. "It's like, I don't know. Like you want to be somebody you're not. I love you the way you are; you know that. I don't know if you did something different with your makeup or what, but you look . . . different."

"I sold my cell phone to the devil to become gorgeous," I explained.

She didn't respond.

After a minute, I said, "Seriously, Jade. I had the weirdest dream the other night—"

She interrupted me. "Fine, Allison. Go ahead. Be sarcastic, fall in love with your own obnoxiousness. Hang with wild Roxanne Green and abandon your true friends. I shouldn't care, I guess, but you've been my best friend for a long time, so I—"

"I wasn't kidding," I tried to explain. "This has been the craziest week, and just now, a woman from *zip* magazine called and said they want me to . . ."

"Allison, stop! Can you quit being ridiculous for one second? I am trying to talk to you. I've been defending you all day and now you're making me wonder if everybody was actually right."

"Right about what?" I asked.

Jade sighed. "I think I owe it to you to tell you people are talking about you, and it isn't pretty."

My call waiting buzzed through. Roxie. I ignored it and sank down deeper into the couch. Everybody was talking about me? Oh, hideousness.

"I wouldn't say anything if I didn't care about you," Jade said.

"I know," I answered, feeling the knot in my stomach tighten again. "I know. What are they saying?"

"Just—you know what, who even cares? That's what my mother said when I told her about it."

"You told your mother?" I knew she told her mother everything, but I mean, please.

"Not the details, don't worry," Jade said, in her talking-me-down voice. "Just, like, the general stuff people were saying about you, because I was so upset. But she was like, 'Allison is your best friend. Don't even listen to all that awful gossip—it will rot your soul.' And I think she has a point, don't you? That kind of talk is just beneath us. You know?"

I didn't know if I knew, so I didn't answer.

"Screw them," Jade said. "They don't know you like I do. You want the homework?"

"Um, yeah, sure," I said, getting out a scrap of paper, since my backpack was still in the bushes. "Thanks, Jade."

"You're welcome," she said, in her near-whisper voice. "You're my best friend. You know I'll always be there for you."

"Yeah," I said. "I know. It's just been a weird week."

"That's exactly what I was telling everybody," Jade

said. " 'Everybody has a weird week at some point. It doesn't mean Allison has changed.' I must have said that twenty times today."

"Thanks." I closed my eyes. "What would I do without you?"

"You'd be lost," she said quietly, and then told me what homework I had to do.

10

By THE TIME THE FORMS arrived on Thursday afternoon, I'd become an expert on mail delivery times. The worst thing, I knew, would be for somebody else to get the mail, read something about my short but apparently impressive modeling career, and then be waiting in the kitchen, with a tapping foot, raised eyebrows, and the documents in hand, when I strolled in from school.

So I'd skipped tennis team practice Tuesday and Wednesday, and by Thursday, the postal officer, Evangeline, and I had become close. Turns out she had a son who was heading off for college in the fall, and he'd been a mail stalker while he waited for decision letters in April. So Evangeline sympathized, and waited while I looked through our stack of bills and junk mail until I found it.

"That what you were waiting for?"

"Yup," I said.

She wished me luck and I sent luck to her son.

So that was nice. I'd spent the week feeling kind of tense and prickly with both Jade and Roxie, but at least I was friends with Evangeline, the mail woman. I almost asked her in for a lemonade.

Another weird but nice thing was that, as I discovered when I sliced open the envelope with a knife in the quiet kitchen, it wasn't at all a misunderstanding. *Zip* magazine had actually chosen me as a semifinalist model.

Me.

Allison Avery. (Okay, Alison Avery, but still.)

The "interesting-looking" Avery girl. The one of me, Jade, and Serena who was most likely to wear the wrong thing, the worst makeup, the fewest hair products—and to care least about it.

Zip magazine thought I was one of the twenty most gorgeous teens in America.

And all I'd had to do was let my cell phone go a little wacky.

Well, that realization whomped me right back down to earth. Obviously it wasn't that I was actually gorgeous; I had cheated. I had sold my cell phone so that a few people would be conned into thinking I was gorgeous. By the devil.

Not that I believed in him.

But maybe I was starting to, because I had to believe either that the devil had magically appeared in my bedroom one night and traded me gorgeousness for my cell phone, or that people whose job it is to recognize gorgeousness chose me as one of the most gorgeous teens in the country.

No contest.

I was dashing up the stairs to hide in my room so I could reread the forms when, as if to emphasize which was real, my cell phone played a series of loud trumpet sounds, had a small seizure, and died.

I scrunched down on the far side of my bed and studied the forms. Before I could compete in the semifinal round of twenty teens, I would need to get a parent to sign a paper filled with small print. The likelihood of that happening was somewhere between *not* and *are you out of your mind*. I read on anyway, just for kicks.

If I won (ha ha ha ha ha), not only would I receive the honor of gracing (yes, "gracing") the cover of the September issue of *zip* magazine, I would also get a boatload of beauty products (bringing up the irony of giving beauty products to the one person who evidently needs them least) and a free trip to the South of France for myself and one parent, for a weeklong photo shoot, and also $10,000.

Not cash, though. A scholarship. That made me almost laugh out loud. If you're gorgeous, you get not just stuff to make you even more stunning, but also *a scholarship*. Because stunning looks prove you are a real scholar, as everybody knows.

A knock on my door made me jump. I was still shoving

the papers into the envelope and the envelope under my bed when Dad loped into my room.

"Hey, Lemon?"

"What!?" I tried to wipe the guilty look off my face. *Open eyes wide for an innocent look,* I remembered reading in one of Phoebe's dumb magazines. Oops, the one I might soon be gracing the cover of.

"What's up?" he asked, his eyes wide, too. Maybe he'd read the same article.

Okay, the thought of Dad thumbing through *zip* was too weird even for me. "Nada," I said slightly frantically. "Just hanging."

He nodded.

I nodded.

I am the child my father borrows books from the library about, searching for ways to not scream at me. Somehow he gets along easily with everybody except me. My mother screams at me, too, but she screams at everybody sometimes. (Well, not Phoebe. Nobody screams at Phoebe; she's the *baby* and so *sweet.*) But Dad, who is the most popular teacher at Willow Brook Elementary, reserves his short fuse only for me.

So I braced myself. Obviously he had found out I'd cut school.

I had no excuse, so I decided to just take whatever he had to dish out and try not to argue back. That's what he had advised me to do the last time I got in huge trouble, for pushing Quinn down the stairs. I had thought it was a good idea to let him know why I had chosen to give her a slight shove, which wouldn't have knocked a sturdier person off balance at all: She had said she would play lacrosse with me in the backyard, so I hauled all the stuff out there, and it had been a really rough day because Jade was mad at me for embarrassing her by laughing too loud at something she'd said in the cafeteria about the smell of tuna, so she and Serena were giving me the silent treatment and I just wanted to whip a ball around. Quinn had said yes and came out after I got everything out there, and then played for, like, five minutes, but then she said she had to go to the bathroom. I waited out there for about half an hour, and when I finally came in to see if she was okay, she was upstairs, reading a book. Apparently she'd had enough lacrosse. So I gave her a slight tap. I was just trying to explain, when Dad was yelling at me, that I had actually shown tremendous restraint by not breaking Quinn's arms off, and maybe he could at least compliment me about that. But no.

He had insisted, fake-calmly, that in the future I should just listen and then apologize.

So that was my plan, when faced with the fact that I had totally ditched school and anyway still had no excuses.

If he knew I also took the train and the subway and let somebody take pictures of me and then gave out our address, I'd be grounded until I was dead.

"How's school?" he asked. *Ah, very tricky,* I thought. Trying to get me to admit what I had done.

Laying the groundwork for an excuse, I said, "Boring."

He nodded.

This was like chess.

"Any clubs or anything interesting?"

"No."

"Other than the tennis team, right?"

Unsure where he was going with that, I said, "Yeah."

"Uh-huh. Still loving that?"

"No," I said. "It sucks."

"Why?" he asked. Probing, probing. But I wasn't falling for it.

"Because it's, like, all about the outfits now. Who has the nicest racquets, who got a new top, who's wearing the same thing she wore to the last match. I mean, is it a team or a fashion show?"

Damn! He was trapping me! Why was I mentioning fashion? I clamped my mouth shut tight.

He nodded. Roxie had said her parents nod too much, but I had never noticed it about mine before. He was a total bobblehead. How annoying and distracting! *Out with it already, Dad,* I was thinking. *Yell at me, punish me, just stop toying with me!*

"I need to talk with you, Allison."

Uh-oh. My real name. Here we go.

"Something happened Monday."

I tried desperately to think of an excuse. *I had to cut school because* . . . *It's not my fault because* . . . Nothing was coming.

"You know what's going on with Mom, and her job . . ."

I shrugged. I knew she was fired, but not that much more in terms of specifics. Was he really going the guilt-trip route? Not his usual style.

"Well, because of that, we're in kind of a bind in terms of cash flow. You know what that means?"

Okay, he was talking to me like I was an idiot kinder-gartner and it made me want to bop him over the head, but actually I *didn't* know what that meant, so I shrugged one shoulder.

He sighed. "We don't have a lot of cash. I don't want you to worry; we'll be okay. It's just that right now, we are in a bind."

"Okay," I said, trying to figure out how this related to me cutting school Monday. My scalp was starting to sweat.

"You understand?"

"Yes, Dad! I am not the idiot you think I am! I follow. We're out of money. In a bind. I get it. Move on!"

His face turned a little red, but he took a breath and then another, the way one of his library books had sug-gested. I read them while he was playing the piano or watching sports on TV, so I would know what he'd be trying on me.

"You won't be able to go to Tennis Europe this summer."

His eyes focused on my beige carpet for a few seconds and then lifted to meet mine. They weren't angry eyes, or accusatory. They looked sad, and kind of apologetic. Weird.

"Did I do something wrong?" I asked. "Am I punished?"

"Not at all, Lemon-head," he said, reaching toward me. Thinking he was trying to grab the letter, which was in fact touching my left pinky toe under the bed, I hid my empty hands behind my back. "Not at all." He dropped his hands and came to sit beside me on my bed, which wrinkled my duvet. "You're not in trouble at all. We are so sorry. But there was a logjam at the bank, apparently, because of some complicated financial maneuverings Mom had to make, which, to be honest, I'm not sure I fully understand myself, and the bottom line is, the payment to Tennis Europe didn't go through."

I surreptitiously shoved the letter a bit farther under the bed.

"We're really sorry, but it looks like you won't be able to go on the trip."

"That's okay," I said.

"I know you and Jade and Serena have been looking

forward to going together, and it was certainly an exciting opportunity . . ."

"Seriously, dude," I said. "It's okay. Don't worry about it."

He shook his head and reached out his arms. Before I knew what he was doing, he had gathered me into a hug. "What a generous person you are, Allison. Thank you."

"It's no big deal," I said. "I don't care about Tennis Europe."

"I know that's not completely true," he said. "But I appreciate your saying it anyway." He let go and looked at me. "You are really growing up so beautifully."

My eyes felt tight, like they might start to cry, so I just looked away and asked, "Is Mom okay?"

"Stressed," he said. "But yes. We'll all be fine. We'll find something good for you for the summer, okay, sweetheart?"

Usually he only calls Phoebe sweetheart. "No problem," I said. "I'll be fine. I'll figure something out." *Like maybe I'll go to the South of France.*

He got up and went to my door. I resisted straightening out my duvet. He smiled at me, so I smiled back, noticing that his lips disappeared, too, and it wasn't so hideous. It was kind of cute.

When he had closed the door, I fixed the duvet and sat back down to reread the *zip* paperwork. Ten thousand dollars if I won. Ten thousand dollars I could give Mom and

Dad. No way Phoebe was making $10,000 this summer, or even Quinn. Ten thousand dollars. I pictured myself handing it over to them, insisting they take it, the whole thing, not even hoarding ten bucks for myself. The whole fat wad of cash, all for them, to help out. To be generous. From their difficult child.

Picturing that was even better than picturing myself on the cover of a magazine I had always—it was true—looked down my (apparently quite lovely) nose at. I grabbed an envelope from the box on my desk and addressed it. My heart was pounding as I reread the forms. Ten thousand dollars. I forged Dad's signature and licked the envelope shut before second thoughts could overtake me.

11

THE NEXT MORNING ON the way to the bus stop, I had the envelope in my hand, which was sweating inside my sweatshirt pocket. Well, it's not like I could have left it overnight in the mailbox with the flag up the way I did when I was little and I left notes out there for the tooth fairy. (I know, I know, you're supposed to leave your tooth under your pillow, but there was no way I could go to sleep thinking some lady was about to fly into my room and take away one of my body parts for a minimal payment—sorry, that's creepy.) First of all, I wasn't completely convinced anybody but the tooth fairy checked the mailbox for outgoing mail, and didn't want to offend Evangeline so early in our friendship. But second and more importantly, one or both of my parents could easily notice the flag up, I realized, and if they went to investigate, I'd be cooked.

So I had to drop the letter in the mailbox halfway up our street toward the bus stop.

My plan was to be up and out early and for once leave without Quinn, but it didn't exactly work out. Phoebe had taken my flip-flops again over the weekend and I had to scrape the muck off them before I could wear them, and then our toaster was freaking out as usual (our appliances have way too much personality), and by the time I was in a sweat and dashing out the door, Quinn was right by my side.

So I decided, as we approached the mailbox, to just be casual. "Oh, Dad asked me to mail this," I said, as if, *What a pain but no big deal,* waving the letter carelessly but quickly so she couldn't read the address. I opened the mailbox door and, as it creaked, flipped the envelope onto it, facedown, and let go fast.

Only, Quinn's hand was on it, holding it open. With her other hand she lifted the letter off. The mailbox creaked shut.

"What is it?"

"How should I know?" I said, a little too high.

"You addressed the envelope," Quinn said, showing it to me.

I raised my eyebrows.

"So . . . ?"

"It's a subscription, if you must know," I lied. "I just decided I need to learn more about, well, fashion. And celebrities. And how to do my makeup. You know. I know I've always made fun of those stupid magazines, so I'm a little embarrassed and didn't want you to know, but . . ."

"It doesn't say *Subscription Department*," Quinn pointed out. "It says *The New Teen Contest*."

"Um," I said. "We're gonna miss the bus if we don't hurry."

"Tell me what this is," Quinn said in her slow, slow way, "or I will rip it open and see for myself."

She lifted her other hand and was starting to rip when I caved.

"Okay, okay. I'll tell you." She froze, waiting to see if I really would tell. "It's that thing I went to with Roxie. They chose me."

"As what?" Quinn asked.

"As a security guard," I said. "What do you think? As a semifinalist."

"Seriously?"

"Thanks for the vote of confidence."

"No, it's not . . . I mean, you're gorgeous, everybody knows that; it's just—"

I had to blink away a surprise tear. "No, I'm not!" I yelled. "Stop mocking me!"

"I'm totally not, Allison," Quinn said. "You're mad beautiful. I mean, you were kind of a weird-looking kid, but you're really coming into yourself these days."

I sniffled and punched her shoulder. "Great, thanks."

"I'm just saying, what did Mom and Dad say? How did you explain it to them?"

"I haven't yet."

We heard the bus rumbling half a block away.

"So what is this?" Quinn asked.

"I just had to fill out a form with my information," I told her half truthfully. "The last thing Mom and Dad need right now is to worry about me, right? It's meaningless. The other girls are all probably, like, professional models. The most that could happen is what? I get a certificate for being a semifinalist?"

"So then why are you doing it?" Quinn asked.

The tears welling up in my eyes caught us both by surprise when I answered, truthfully for once, "Because I never get the certificate."

"Oh, Allison," Quinn said, softening.

"You have no idea how that feels, Quinn." I sniffed hard and collected myself. "Can you put it in the mailbox so we don't miss the bus, please? I really don't want to push my luck and be late."

Quinn frowned. She has never been late in her life. She sighed and opened the mailbox. Before she placed the envelope in, though, she lifted it to her lips and kissed it. "For luck," she whispered.

"Thanks," I managed, and then we sprinted toward the bus together.

It wasn't until Jade and Serena were on their way onto the bus at the next stop that I realized I was going to have to come up with something to tell them about why I wouldn't be going with them to Tennis Europe. It hit me that I should've come up with a story ahead of time, but honestly, how much deception can I be expected to plan in one night?

Jade must have seen my face looking shocked, because her face morphed from her usual look of determined innocence to one of concern, and she slipped right in beside me. "What's wrong, Allison?"

I opened my mouth but for once nothing came out.

"Did they find out you ditched school?"

"Yes," I told her, secretly thanking her for solving my problem.

"How?" Serena asked from across the aisle.

"I don't know," I admitted, panicking afresh. "How could they have found out?"

"Maybe the school called," Jade whispered. "Or one of the teachers who's friends with your dad."

"Right," I agreed. "That must be it."

Jade shook her head. "I told you, Allison. I don't know why you did that. It's so not like you. So what did they do? How much trouble are you in?"

It was almost hard not to grin, this was going so well. I could keep my family's business and my own all private without breaking a sweat. I really am the Fort Knox of secrets, I congratulated myself, while saying, "Large trouble."

Serena leaned into the aisle, her elbows on her knees.

As a soap opera addict, she had to be in heaven with this.

"I'm out of Tennis Europe."

"No!" Serena and Jade both gasped.

I nodded sadly.

"That's so harsh!" Serena said.

"She cut school for the whole day," Jade said. "We're in ninth grade, Serena; this isn't baby stuff anymore. You cut school for one day and you could totally wreck your college chances. It could go on your transcript. You think the competitive colleges want someone who just ditches school?"

"Whoa," Serena said, and I thought.

"I mean, it stinks, but can you really blame Allison's parents? She's lucky she's not suspended." She turned to me with a disappointed look on her pretty oval face. "Where did you and Roxanne Green go, anyway? I hope it was worth it."

"It kind of was," I couldn't help saying, especially because in truth I actually hadn't suffered any consequences. Maybe I'd feel different if I'd really been caught and screwed up my whole future, which would probably be murky at best even without radically stupid moves on my part like cutting school. Still, the more I thought about not being able to do Tennis Europe, the more relieved I felt. It was weird, because I'd begged to be allowed to go only a few months earlier, and now it felt like a too-small hat had suddenly been removed from my head.

The bus was pulling up to school by then, so we grabbed our stuff and trudged off toward the side entrance of school.

"So?" Jade asked again. "Why aren't you telling us where you went when you cut?"

"I already told you," I said as we approached Jade's locker. "We went into the city."

"By yourselves?" Serena asked, shocked.

"Yeah. Roxie used to model, and—"

"She really did?" Serena asked. "I thought that was just a rumor."

"Rumors aren't always false," Jade murmured.

"Cool," Serena said, sounding, as always, vaguely astonished.

"She's done commercials and catalogues, lots of stuff," I told them as Jade completed her morning locker-crap-sorting ritual. "Anyway, we went to this open call for models for this magazine called *zip*."

"I *love zip*!" Serena shrieked. When she caught Jade's condemnatory look, she continued in a forced whisper, "Well, it's the hottest magazine, isn't it? Roxie is in *zip*?"

Roxie flumped up just then, and said, "Apparently not."

I looked at her and she half smiled back. "No call," she said. "So, I guess I wasn't moe again."

"Who's moe?" Serena asked.

"Inside joke," Roxie said, and I caught the split-second

107

tightening in Jade's face. Roxie apparently didn't, because she just forged right ahead, saying, "I don't know if Allison told you guys, but we went to try out for this cover-model contest, the New Teen or something. There were probably close to a thousand girls there, don't you think?"

I shrugged. Jade and Serena were looking from Roxie to me and back like we were aliens.

"They would've called by yesterday if we'd made the next round. Did they call you, Allison?"

"No," I lied.

"Me neither," she said. "So I guess that's that. Oh, well, I still think we're gorgeous, don't you?"

I half shrugged, half shook my head. Jade made a disgusted clucking sound as she rearranged her books at the bottom of her perfectly neat locker. She cannot tolerate bragging.

"Anyway," Roxie continued, either oblivious to or ignoring all the little psychodramas she was causing, "I'm kind of down in the dumps about it and thinking, What the hell, it's Memorial Day weekend and I have no plans and nothing exciting going on, so do you guys want to make it a party Saturday night? Or we could do Sunday, whatever; I'm flexible. My parents are going to Bermuda with clients."

"Um," Serena said. She and—I have to admit—I both looked at Jade to see how she'd respond.

She smiled. "That sounds great, Roxanne," Jade said

evenly. "But unfortunately Allison and Serena are coming with my family to our place in Sag Harbor." She turned to check her lip gloss in the little round mirror she had affixed to her locker door.

"Oh, well." Roxie shrugged. "It was an idea. Have fun, then, you three."

Just as she was turning away, I said, "Actually, I'm not going."

All three of my friends looked shocked, although once again I may have been the surprise winner in the who-did-I-shock-most contest.

"Grounded," I explained.

Jade put her arm around my shoulder and said, "Oh, Allison."

I closed my eyes, feeling almost as terrible as I was pretending to feel.

"She got caught cutting," Jade was explaining to Roxie. "You didn't get a call from the school?"

"She had permission," I said quickly.

"Oh, Double Shot, that totally sucks," Roxie said. "When did your parents find out? Who called?"

Uh-oh, I thought, but said, "They wouldn't say." I kept my eyes closed and felt Jade's arm tighten around me. She smelled, as always, clean and shiny from her floral shampoo.

"Your mother lets you just skip school and go into the city for the day?"

Roxie half shrugged and nodded at the same time. "I guess."

Jade slid her eyes away, making it clear what she thought of Roxie's mother's parenting philosophy. "Well, this school takes stuff like unnecessary absences and cutting really seriously," Jade explained quietly. "You really have to be careful. You don't want to be one of those girls who just foolishly throws away her future."

As Jade was leading me away, with Serena fast at her heels, I heard Roxie, behind us, saying, "No. I want to be one of those girls who throws away her future with brilliant forethought."

In spite of myself, I had to smile. Just a little bit, and mostly on the inside.

12

WHEN I WAS YOUNGER, I used to wish my mom would be around more, like other kids' mothers. On playdates, their moms would sit at the kitchen table and ask us about our day and give us cookies or even sandwiches with the crusts cut off. At my house, no crusts were cut off and a snack was laid out by Gosia, our housekeeper, and it was sliced apples and cheese. Nobody asked about our day.

It wasn't that I ever thought Mom was a bad mother or a slacker. I was actually very proud that she, like other kids' dads, rode the train in to work and held the *Wall Street Journal* folded into a little origami square and read the hieroglyphics streaming across the bottom of the news on TV. I loved that she could walk faster in heels than other moms in their Merrills on the rare occasions she made it to a class breakfast, and it truly didn't bother me that I usually had to read my haiku first because she'd need to slip out ASAP to get to her office.

But part of me did wish I could, once in a while, have her around when I got home from school and she would ask me what happened in my day and she would just know what my plans were for the weekend.

I had no idea how weird and invasive that would feel until I got home that Friday afternoon.

Figuring I had basically quit the tennis team, I took the early bus home by myself and wandered up the street feeling let loose on the world. After tennis practice, I knew, Jade and Serena would rush home to shower and pack, and then Jade's parents would drive around the corner to pick Serena up. Jade's little brother, Kyle, would be watching a movie or playing with one of his million little electronic games in one of the captain seats in the second row, leaving the back bench for Jade, Serena, and me—but I wouldn't be there. I wasn't worried that Jade's parents would call mine to discuss my grounding; they were friendly, but not friends, with my parents now, and, like Jade, painfully appropriate and wary about social issues.

I had no plans at all.

There were probably parties planned all over town for those few who weren't heading out to the Hamptons, and twice as many parties out there, but of course I wasn't invited to any of them. I waited for the pain and self-loathing of that realization to hit me, but for once it didn't. I could lie in bed all weekend and read if I wanted, or watch TV, maybe a marathon of Hitchcock movies. I used to live in fear of having no friends and being invisible, but right then it seemed like an okay possibility.

I walked up my driveway actually whistling, until I realized I must seem (if anybody were looking at me) like a refugee from a 1950s movie.

What a dork.

When I opened the door, Mom was there, smiling, in socks and sweats. I almost jumped out of my skin. When she said, "Hi, cutie! How was your day?" I actually turned and looked behind me, wondering who she might mean. Nobody there. Then I thought maybe I'd come to the wrong house, or was dreaming again.

"What's wrong?" I finally asked.

"Nothing," she said. "Don't you have tennis practice?"

I was still on the step, but the freezing wave of air-conditioning was wafting over me, which might (or might not) explain my sudden wooziness. "I quit," I said.

"Oh," Mom answered. "All righty then. You want a snack?"

"Who are you and what have you done with my mother?" I asked, not budging.

Mom laughed.

I didn't.

"Are you the devil?" I asked, trying to get a look at her eyes.

"Allison, come in and shut the door," she snapped.

"You are letting out all the air-conditioning."

I breathed a sigh of relief and followed her toward the kitchen, shutting the door behind me.

On the counter was a new bikini and a bottle of sunblock. She smiled tensely beside them. "I think it's your size," she said. "I hope so. And this is the sunblock you like, right?"

I nodded.

"For your weekend," she explained. "Aren't you going away with Jade's family this weekend?"

"No," I answered.

Her tense smile faded. "It was on the calendar."

She looked so disappointed, I almost gave her a hug. That would've been weird. Instead I assured her, "Oh, it was the plan. I just . . . I told her I couldn't go."

"Why?" Mom asked. "It's not because of my . . . situation at work, is it? Are you worried about spending money? Because this is just a temporary setback, Allison. I don't want you to—"

"No," I interrupted. "No. It's just . . . we're not . . . Jade has been kind of annoying me lately."

"Really?" she asked, sounding genuinely concerned. "In what way? Tell me what's been going on with you." She sat down on one of the counter stools and cocked her head, ready to listen.

It completely freaked me out.

It was the exact thing I had pictured whenever I wished for her to be around more. It was my secret fantasy come true.

I hated it.

"I don't know," I said, turning away and passing by the plate of cookies on the counter. I opened the fridge and grabbed a can of Diet Coke. "So, anyway, I hope it doesn't mess up your plans to have me around this weekend. You can just ignore me."

"Not at all, Allie Cat," she said. Okay, I was officially freaked. She hadn't called me Allie Cat since I was in third grade.

"I gotta go get a head start on my homework," I told her, heading fast for the back stairs before she, like, kissed me or something. "Big project to work on."

I took the stairs by twos.

My cell phone buzzed as I was crossing the upstairs den.

It was a text from Roxie:

I know u'r grounded but can you still use your cell and IM?

I texted back:

Can u keep a secret?

Yes, she sent back immediately. *Like u. Absolutely.*

In my room by then, I flopped down on my couch and texted:

I'm not really grounded. I just couldn't stand the idea of being stuck with them all wknd. Is that horrible? They r my best friends.

It took a minute or two for her to respond, during which time I made long mental lists of why I am a terrible person. But then I read her message:

Not anymore. I am ur BFF now.

I read that about twenty times, and then texted back, *True.*

13

MY PARENTS WERE PROWLING our halls, trying to cheer us up and reassure us (which I must say is the most worry-making thing parents can do to their kids) in between long sessions of going over papers in the study. Friday night, Quinn and I watched TV in my room for a while and fell asleep in a tangle of blankets and pillows like we used to when we were little. But when I woke up Saturday morning she was gone, and after both my parents repeatedly asked me how I was doing, I realized I had to get out of there, too.

I texted Roxie and when she said, *Absolutely come over right now!*, I was packed and out the door within ten minutes.

I slept at Roxie's Saturday night and we found out from Facebook and various other sources where everybody was headed party-wise. We counted ourselves lucky to be out of it and settled in front of the TV with pints of

Ben & Jerry's frozen yogurt.

"Maybe *we* should have a party," Roxie suggested during one commercial break.

"I think we're having it," I told her. "All the guests who would come are already here."

"Oh," Roxie said, and laughed.

Next commercial break, she said, "It totally makes no sense at all for me to be depressed about not making the callback for *zip*."

"They made a mistake," I said, meaning more than she knew.

She turned and smiled at me. "You're the best."

There was nothing she could have said that would have made me feel worse. "No, really. I suck."

She laughed out loud. "You just think you suck."

"I'm pretty sure. I've known me for a long time."

She laughed again but then interrupted herself. "You know what?"

"What?"

"Let's crash that party tomorrow night."

"The one at the girl's house? Madeleine freaking Smith? We don't even really know her. It'll be all, like, seniors." There was no way I was going to that party.

Twenty hours later we were in Roxie's huge bathroom, getting ready to go to the party.

I already felt so guilty for getting her *zip* spot (I knew it made no sense really to think that, but I couldn't help it) and also for not telling her about it (which was so wrong and I knew it, it's just that it would've been even more wrong to tell her and probably it would amount to nothing, so why make her feel worse?) that I had to do anything she wanted to make up for it.

With family I am all, "Screw you." With friends I chase myself around in circles trying to make it up to them.

I sat down on the stool next to Roxie's while she pulled her hair back in a headband to start her makeup. She casually threw a spare, still in the wrapping, to me. I pretty much gave up makeup at the beginning of ninth grade, after using way too much eyeliner in eighth. I often came home from middle school looking like a raccoon, despite Jade's sign-language indications to me to wipe beneath my eyes. Jade said I looked better without eye makeup anyway. More innocent. Just a little lip gloss, she recommended because of my lip issue, and waterproof mascara for special occasions. Jade thought I should de-emphasize my eyes so I wouldn't look so much like an alien. Thus the long bangs I cut for myself. Nothing de-emphasizes eyes like not seeing them.

But I slipped Roxie's spare headband on, for something to do, and tried not to make eye contact with myself in the mirror. Instead I searched around pointlessly through her limitless supply of makeup.

"You want to do smoky eyes?" Roxie asked. "I downloaded a how-to yesterday." She opened the laptop on the counter beside her and clicked on a clip of a makeup artist talking about what she was doing to some girl's eyelids.

I did whatever she described, left eye then right, left then right, painting my face as if it were a canvas in art class: thick line, smudge it, blend toward the crease. Shadow, highlight, blend. Curl the lashes with the medieval torture device, then mascara, two coats.

"Wow," Roxie said, when the how-to ended.

I checked myself out in the mirror. I didn't look familiar, or not completely. I looked older, harder, tougher.

I liked it.

I picked up a concealer and dabbed it under my eyes and around my nostrils, then spread some tinted moisturizer over my forehead, chin, and cheeks.

"Red lips, I think," Roxie suggested, handing me a tray of choices. I lined my lips in the reddest pencil I could find and then filled them in.

"Holy crap," Roxie said. "Who the heck are you?"

"No idea," I answered from behind the mask.

"I think maybe the devil went beyond his side of the bargain. Nobody could think you're anything BUT gorgeous."

"You're just a good friend," I told her, feeling myself blush beneath the makeup.

"I am that," she said, her bright blue eyes all sparkly within her smoky-eyed makeup, and turned back to add some gloss to her pouty lips.

"Roxie," I started, determined to come clean and just tell her I'd gotten the callback.

She stood up abruptly. "But meanwhile, what are you going to wear to go with all that gorgeousness?"

I sat on the edge of Roxie's bed while she started tearing things out of her closet. After a few false starts, we settled on a tank dress of hers with a tiny cardigan. She wore a tight T-shirt and a short skirt with boots. We stood in front of the mirror in her front hall, sticking out our tongues at our hot selves.

"We are absolutely gorgeous," Roxie gushed. "We are clean-cut but with an edge. That dumb magazine missed out, I tell you."

My stomach was churning as we piled into the backseat of her housekeeper's car to get driven to the party. On our way there, with Roxie singing along to a "get-psyched" song, as she called it, I made a promise to myself: *Tonight, I will pretend to be somebody who has fun at parties.*

We could hear the music blaring from down the block, where we got Roxie's housekeeper to drop us off. Despite the fact that it was still warm out, I shivered as we waited on the top step for the front door to open. A senior guy with broad shoulders and a spiky 'do flung open the door and, waving his big red plastic cup toward the kitchen, announced, "Come in, come in!" Beer sloshed out behind him, narrowly missing a dark ponytail that swung away just in time, its owner putting on a pout before getting engulfed in the big guy's thick arm.

"Are we the only ninth graders here?" I whispered to Roxie.

"Let's go," she answered, or didn't, dragging me toward the kitchen.

I reminded myself to pretend I was somebody else, somebody gorgeous and fun, and followed her. Within a couple of seconds there was a red plastic cup in my hand and two guys, one on either side of me, vying for my attention.

It was surreal.

I lost track of Roxie pretty fast, but looking for her gave me something to do. I smiled with my lips closed at the two guys and left. Behind me I heard one of them ask the other, "Who *was* that?" and made a silent prayer not to let those two Neanderthals eat up my allotment of admirers. I only had five or maybe four more to go, if you counted somebody making decisions at *zip*. I obviously couldn't afford to waste any on partially evolved boys.

Just as I spotted Roxie across what was either the family room or the living room of Madeleine Smith's highly decorated, vibrating house, my arm was touched.

"Allison Avery?"

I turned to look right at Tyler Moss.

"Tyler Moss," I said.

"Having fun?" he asked.

"I always do," I lied.

"Yeah," he said with that crooked smile just starting. "Me neither."

"Hello," said Jade, beside him, unsmiling.

Her smooth brown hair was pulled back in a low pony-tail, and her pale pink lipstick glinted in the dim light. She looked, as always, exactly the way I would want to look.

"Hi," I answered, willing myself not to sound shaky. "What are you doing here?"

"I think I should ask you the same thing." Jade raised her perfectly tweezed eyebrows and scanned my outfit, down then up. I forced myself not to gather the suddenly even skimpier cardigan over my nonexistent chest. Jade didn't have smoky eyes, far from it. She had only her mascara, and was wearing a white short-sleeved button-down with a very cute light blue flared skirt.

Clearly sensing the tension despite his boyness, Tyler asked us, "You two know each other? Jade Demarchelier, Allison Avery?"

"We used to," Jade answered.

"Why aren't you in Sag Harbor?" I asked, remembering that Serena's older sister was best friends with Madeleine freaking Smith. Ugh.

"We came back early because my grandmother got sick," Jade answered so coldly icicles formed around the words. "I texted you."

"You did?"

"Yes, twice, and called you. I left three messages on your voice mail. I was really upset about my grandmother and needed you."

I grabbed my phone. As soon as it was in my hand, the *You have voice mail* chimes went off. I looked: three new voice mails, two text messages.

"I'm sorry," I said. "I never heard—"

"I figured maybe your parents took your phone away," she practically growled. "Aren't you grounded?"

"Oh. Yes," I spluttered.

"So you snuck out?"

"Kind of," I said.

Jade shook her head slowly.

My phone played a short series of high-pitched bird screeches and went dead in my hand. Not feeling up to explaining it, I asked Jade, "How's your grandmother?"

"Better, thank you for asking," she said formally. My cheeks felt frostbitten as I slipped my dead phone back into my clutch. "You're looking . . . different," Jade added, moving her gaze to my other hand, the one holding the beer cup.

"I am different," I lied.

"So I see," Jade agreed, and then, clearly done with me, flicked her flirty eyes up at Tyler and blinked them twice. "Anyway, Tyler, what were—"

"I think I need some air," I said, turning away from them. No way was she dismissing me, not again, not in front of Tyler Moss, not with me wearing my mask of invincibility. I was a jerk. Fine. I never thought anything better of myself than that. I didn't need her shoving my face in it, was all.

I was maybe two steps away, stretching my fingers to dispel their sudden numbness, when I heard Tyler, behind me, say, "I'll go with you."

I didn't trust myself to turn around, no matter how much I wanted to see the look on Jade's face. I could feel him following me through and then out of the house.

We walked side by side up Madeleine Smith's walk as I poured out my stinky untouched beer in her bushes. I tossed my cup in her trash can and we took a left onto the sidewalk, still without a word. It was only when we rounded the corner that I said, "Now she'll hate me more than ever."

"Jade? Why?" Tyler asked.

"We're best friends."

"But you just said—"

"I just keep disappointing her. Because I am a screwup and she is perfect. Are you going out with her?"

"No," he said. "I'm not going out with anybody. How about you?"

"No," I said. After that we didn't talk again for a while.

"You leave places abruptly," he observed, finally.

I shrugged. "I have bad manners."

"Manners are overrated."

"Yours are good."

"You don't know me very well," he said, and put his arm around me. Next thing I knew he was kissing me.

We had stopped just in the rim of light from a street lamp, so our faces were half-bright, half-shadowed. I didn't wrap my arms around him, but I didn't pull away either, until I felt him start to.

My first kiss.

I found it a bit hard to breathe during it. It was equally hard to breathe after.

"You're right," I managed. "That was pretty rude."

His cheeks burned red instantly, and he blinked hard twice. "I'm sorry," he said. "I'm . . . I'm sorry."

"No. I was just making a . . . That's not . . . Don't be," I said. "Except for the . . . I don't think red is your color, lipstick-wise."

His fingers flew up to his lips and rubbed until all traces of the kiss were obliterated. "Yeah, well . . ." he started.

I turned away. He wasn't going to reject me, either. No way, not tonight, and not right after being the first boy to ever kiss me. "I should get back," I said, and started walking back toward the party.

He caught up by the corner. "You're pretty fast," he said.

"No," I countered. "Just quick."

"Can I call you?" he asked, producing his cell phone out of his pocket and handing it to me.

"My phone is dead," I said, keying in my number. "Either that or possessed by the devil."

"Right," he answered, taking the phone back and pressing one button. "Either that or you just gave me a fake number. Let's see."

I felt my phone vibrate in my clutch, so I dug it out and answered, turning my back to him. "Hello?"

His back pressed up against mine as he said, "I guess you didn't lie."

"I never lie," I lied.

"Me neither," he said. Lied? How to know?

We leaned against each other and didn't say anything for a couple of breaths. Eventually I thought, *Somebody has to say something*, so I asked brilliantly, "How's it going?"

"Hard to say," he said. "There's this girl . . . I just kissed her?"

"Yeah?" I said, feeling the giggles rise in my throat.

"And I can't tell if it was the right thing to do or the stupidest thing ever."

"Did she kiss you back?" I asked.

"Um," he said. "I think so."

"Do you want to kiss her again?"

He breathed out, or maybe laughed one *ha*, and whispered, "Yes."

"Why?"

"Why?" His back pulled away from mine. I cursed silently, a nice variety of curses and self-criticisms, in the two seconds it took him to go on. "Um, I don't know. Because it was . . . nice? And she's smart, independent, funny . . . "

". . . -looking?"

"No," he said immediately. "She's gorgeous. I just don't know . . . if . . ."

And then, nothing. I turned around to see what he was doing when I couldn't stand waiting anymore, and he was standing there with questioning eyes, his phone down at his side. I lowered mine, too, took two steps toward him, and got my second-ever kiss.

14

WHEN TY AND I WALKED back into the party holding hands, everybody turned to look at us. His hand was kind of sweaty, which sounds gross but it wasn't. The guy who had sat on my leg accidentally a few days earlier yelled, "Ty! Where were you, man?"

"Out," Ty said.

The guy looked at me and, grinning, said, "Oh. Hi. I'm Emmett."

"Allison," I said.

A light dawned behind his cute, scrubbed-looking face. "The governor!"

"Right," I said. Ty squeezed my hand.

Even after Roxie came over to us and grinned at me, Ty and I kept holding hands. Even after Jade huffed past us, followed by Serena, with their eyes not quite averted, we didn't let go. Not until Roxie looked at her watch and gasped that her housekeeper would be waiting at the corner, then chugged her beer and tossed the cup in the trash can, did we let go.

"I'll, uh, call you," Ty said.

"Good," I answered, and followed Roxie out into the cool night.

He didn't call.

I kept my phone in my hand all night, and must have checked it a hundred times, a thousand.

When it rang at 11 a.m. my heart almost flew out through my mouth, but it was just my mother asking where I was. I told her I was still at Roxie's and I would be home soon and no, I didn't have much homework. It was weird to have her want so many details.

My phone was silent from then until after dinner. Poor Phoebe had gotten roped into going fishing with Dad. She had been kind of abandoned by me and Quinn all weekend, I realized, as I watched her pushing her food around the plate with her fork, looking bereft, alone, and seasick no matter how much we complimented her on the deliciousness of the bluefish. She had always seemed so happy and cute before; it was kind of heartbreaking to see her in such a weird funk. It made me want to do anything to cheer her up. So what if boys she didn't even like and had never kissed called her all the time and the one boy I had ever really liked or kissed was totally blowing me off?

Hmm. I had lost track of why I was trying to make

myself be sweet to Phoebe. As I cleared my plate, my phone rang.

I vowed that if it was Tyler, I'd be nice to Phoebe for the rest of my life. Or at least the rest of the week.

I closed my eyes and took a breath before I looked and saw it was Roxie. Instead of saying hello, I groaned.

"Well," she said. "That answers my first question."

"How am I going to deal with school tomorrow?" I moaned, heading upstairs.

"He didn't say he'd call *today*," Roxie said. "He might have meant during the week. He looked really happy, standing there holding your hand."

"Really?"

"I swear it," she said. "You are the cutest couple."

"You are the best friend," I said, and my stomach sank.

"Do you think I should like Emmett?"

"Do you?" I asked, surprised. Emmett was sweet, but not especially gorgeous. When I'd liked him, I was embarrassed about it.

"Kind of," Roxie whispered.

"Yes!" I shouted, surprising us both. Quieter, I added, "But only if Ty still likes me."

"It's a deal," Roxie said.

"I was just kidding. You should so like him, if you like him."

"Hey," Roxie said. "I am a big believer in solidarity."

"Ungh," I managed.

Not noticing my tumble into despair, Roxie went on. "Anyway, Ty is going to be head over heels for you tomorrow, so it's not much of a sacrifice on my part. Do you know that this is the first weekend since we moved here that hasn't completely sucked for me? And right when I got rejected from my favorite magazine. Go figure."

"Yeah," I said sinking further down in the devil's seat, feeling bad about myself in every conceivable way.

"You sound bad," Roxie said after a little while.

"I am bad," I answered.

"Here's what you are going to do," she said. "Are you listening?"

"Mmm-hmmm."

"Do you have anything red?"

"Just my phone."

"You need to wear something red," Roxie said. "Everybody knows when you wear red, you look hot. Red is the ultimate screw-you color."

I let out a little laugh.

"You have to wear red, and look your absolute, most drop-dead best, when a boy you thought was going to call you doesn't. You know what the best revenge is, right?"

"Looking good," I whispered.

"That's right. Are you looking in your closet? What do you have that's hot? No neutrals."

"I'm all about neutrals," I moaned.

"No, you've just been hiding your light under a bushel. Come on, Double Shot. Rally!"

"Hiding my what under a what?"

"My grandma says that. You know what else she says?"

"I'm afraid to hear," I admitted, getting off my butt and heading toward my closet.

"You've gotta put the bread in the window."

"Bread?"

"Think about it. What do they do at a bakery? Do they hide the merchandise under neutral sacks? Or do they display it?"

"Bread is neutral-colored," I pointed out, digging toward the back of my closet, stuff I hadn't worn since last summer, stuff Jade and Serena and I had decided was "a little much."

"You know what I mean," Roxie said. "Hot. Red. And you have to do the smoky eyes. Are you taking notes?"

I laughed. "The thing is, Roxie, in all honesty, I'm not hot. I'm not gorgeous. And acting like I think I am will just be humiliating."

"Okay, for one thing, you *are* gorgeous. You just usually do everything you can to convince everybody, including yourself, that you aren't."

"I wish that were true," I moaned.

"It is, but if you don't know it, that's okay. In that case you just have to fake it."

"But that's—"

"Haven't you ever faked sleep?" Roxie interrupted. "Like, when your parents were coming home and you stayed up late with a babysitter or something?"

"About a million times," I admitted. "Sure."

"And what happens if you have to fake sleeping for a while?"

I thought for a few seconds. "I don't know. I usually fall asleep, I guess."

"Exactly," she said. "So, what do you have that's red?"

By the time I hung up with her I was, if not psyched for the next day, at least down off the ledge, with a pile of non-neutral T-shirts to try on stacked beside my bed.

I set my alarm for six so I'd have time to put myself together to Roxie's specifications, forcing the thoughts out of my head about how much I didn't deserve her as a friend. I hadn't purposefully stolen her dream, and probably nothing was going to come of it anyway. Besides, I had to focus. If I was going to get revenge and look gorgeous in front of not just Tyler Moss, who didn't call me, but also Jade and Serena, who hadn't either, it was going to take all my concentration.

15

No hiding today, I told myself as I leaned close to my reflection to line my eyes with darkest brown kohl. If I have too wide a space between my eyes, if my lips get shy, if my nose is too long and skinny, my eyebrows too dark for my coloring, my big freckle above my lip too prominent, my teeth too big, my thighs too thundering . . . well, that's what I look like. No hiding today.

I curled my eyelashes and stroked mascara over them. Figures the blondest thing on me would be my eyelashes. How useless is blond there?

I decided against smoky eyes, just going for a lighter "day" look. Okay, I had studied the *Makeup Tips!* section of the old copy of *zip* I still kept hidden under my bed. *You want a light touch for day,* I reminded myself. Of all things, nerdy me, who for so long had just barely passed as a nice, smart girl instead of a sinking-to-the-probably-more-appropriate status of outcast freak, was now attempting to ascend to the level of hot girl.

Can we just pause and admit that this will never work? I asked my reflection. My reflection, alas (!), ignored me.

So I made a quick prayer that I wouldn't make a complete ass of myself as I spread the pink lip gloss Jade had given me over a copper lipstick I'd bought last year but never used after Jade said it wasn't my color. *Nice girls don't wear more than a sheer lip gloss and maybe a soft coat of mascara to school,* Jade had whispered to me when we first caught a glimpse of Roxie, last fall. I had agreed, then rubbed off my blush on my way to math.

Well, I'm not nice, I told myself as I dabbed cover-up around my nostrils. Why hide it?

"Holy . . ." Quinn said, when she saw me.

"Too much?" I asked, ready to run back to my room and wash it all off, or at least tug my hair down in front to hide.

Quinn studied my face, judging it.

"Quinn!" I yelled.

"No, no. You look good," she said. "Really good. But why?"

I tried not to roll my eyes. Failed. "You know Tyler Moss?"

"Yeah. Jock? Hottie?"

"Exactly. Well—"

"You like him! I knew it! You denied it but—"

"I kissed him Sunday night," I whispered. Quinn

shrieked but slapped her hand over her mouth in time to stifle it.

"Twice."

"Shut up!" she screamed under her hand, and did a weird little . . . well, I think it was a celebratory dance. Or else she really had to pee.

"The thing is," I continued, "he said he'd call but he didn't."

"Oh," Quinn said, catching her breath and returning to her usual pale color from hot pink. She nodded. "Okay. I get it. Red."

"Does everybody know that rule except me?" I asked, heading down to breakfast.

"You apparently know it, too," Quinn said.

Before I could answer I saw Phoebe, already in the kitchen and looking blotchy for the first time in her life. I'd been planning to wear my flip-flops, but there they were, on Phoebe's feet again. But I couldn't even bring myself to yell at her to get them off. The poor kid looked like a wreck, and was getting Gosia to drive her to school, making some excuse about having an early meeting.

It had to be something about having to cancel her graduation party. Her friends were probably giving her hell. If it was going to help her to wear my flip-flops, fine. I tried to ask her if she was okay but she skittered away, eyes averted. Probably she was still mad Quinn and I hadn't solved the problem for her the other day. Still, I felt sorry for her. Well, sorry enough to let her go with my new flip-flops.

I put on my black low-top Chucks instead. No socks. I wasn't sure if black counted as neutral, but it was them or sandals, and as much as I wanted to look screw-you hot, there was no way I was going to school in heels.

Light blue shorts and a red T-shirt were enough.

Plus makeup. Plus hair. I was more put-together than I'd ever been on a school day in my life.

It was also the first time I hadn't cringed, looking at myself in the mirror, since I was maybe ten.

I stood in front of Mom, who was messing with her BlackBerry, and telling Quinn about whatever meeting she had. I wanted to see if Mom would be one of the seven people who would think I was gorgeous. Or if she was immune to me, and the devil, too.

If she was ever going to think I was gorgeous, I thought, it would be right now. I took a breath and relaxed my face, waiting.

Eventually she looked up and noticed me, behind Quinn. "What?" she asked. "If you need some breakfast, you have to get it yourself. I have a billion things—"

"I don't need anything," I said, but didn't budge.

"See you later," Mom said, opening her laptop.

Doubt it, I thought, following Quinn, as always, out the door.

★ ★ ★

Roxie took the bus, for the first time in forever, and was waiting for us at the bus stop when we got there. She and Quinn got into a whole thing of complimenting me that was so embarrassing that if the bus had been another minute late, I would've just turned around and walked home.

Roxie took the aisle seat. I scrunched down next to the window. She yanked my arm and whispered, "Be tall and proud. Just keep two, no, four words in your head all day: *I'm gorgeous and screw you.*"

"That's five," I argued.

She thought for a second and then said, "You can forget the *and*. *I'm gorgeous. Screw you.*"

We were still laughing when Jade and Serena got on, so we had to catch our breath to say hello. They both did double takes, and Serena even smiled a bit at me, but they didn't say anything. They sat down in the seat behind us and started whispering. I sank lower in my seat.

Roxie elbowed me, then stood up, turned around, and kneeled, peering over the back of our seat at Jade and Serena. Their whispering stopped, of course.

"So," Roxie said. "Can you believe this heat?"

"Mm," Jade murmured, noncommittal.

"Good thing I put on a double layer of deodorant this morning or I'd already have big sweat moons showing through my T-shirt. How about you, Jade? You put on enough deodorant this morning? Serena doesn't look like that much of a sweaty person, are you, Serena?"

"Not really, no," Serena answered, sweet and squeaky. I had slumped lower in my seat, but I knew the look Jade was giving her. I had no doubt that was the last thing we'd hear Serena say that morning.

"But you, Jade," Roxie continued. "I bet you can sweat good and stinky, right? You and me, we could stink up a boys' locker room."

"Speak for yourself," Jade quietly answered.

"Yeah, but I put on a double layer, myself," Roxie said. "It's you who's got the sweat moons."

Roxie plopped back down next to me. I half expected her to start snorting and laughing, and my stomach clenched again.

Instead she leaned close to me and whispered, "The silent treatment is mean. She could say hello."

Then she sat back and stuck her buds into her ears and rocked out a bit in our seat.

I watched the town go by backward as we approached school, thinking that maybe the weirdest thing in my life was not that I was wearing a tight red T-shirt and makeup to school, or that I was (secretly) a semifinalist for a magazine modeling competition, or even that the devil had taken possession of my cell phone (which, at that moment, began to play "Pop Goes the Weasel" incessantly at top volume despite all my attempts to shut the thing off), but that Roxie Green really was my best friend.

★ ★ ★

I'm not sure if it was the hair, or the T-shirt, or the makeup, or the whole selling my cell to the devil—or if it was maybe the fact that I was taking longer steps to keep up with Roxie as we sauntered through the halls—but for the first time in my life, people noticed me. I saw eyes focus on me as we approached, and mouths smile as we got near. More kids said, "Hey," or, "What's up," to me than in the whole year put together.

A couple of times in class my cell phone beeped and buzzed, but no teachers yelled at me about it. I just kept it in my back pocket and sat on it. After second period, when it was doing a samba in my shorts, I took it out and read a text from Tyler:

Hey

So I texted back:

Hey

Okay, so it wasn't *Shall I compare thee to a summer's day*, but I was still pretty psyched, and, if I didn't know me, I would say I might have been smiling as I walked into French class.

At lunch, Roxie and I strolled around the fields, arms linked. I hesitated as we came to the upper field where the boys were playing football, but Roxie yanked me on and yelled, "Hey, Ty," as we passed.

He looked at her, then at me, and stopped. He smiled, then frowned, then got hit in the chest with the football and said, I think, "Oof."

"Moss, come on, man!" Emmett yelled at him, but then followed his eyes toward us. Roxie waved at him and he blushed right up. "Oh, hi," he said, standing next to Tyler.

"Head in the game, dumb-asses," another guy yelled at them, shoving them both after picking up the ball.

Roxie turned me and we walked on. We did three laps around the field before we finally sat down on the far end under a huge hemlock tree to eat our lunches.

On our way back in, at least three girls gave me compliments about my hair, and one, Susannah Millstein, who is president of the class every year and plays first singles on the tennis team even though, like me, she is only in ninth grade, made a point of coming over to ask why I had quit tennis.

"I just have so much going on," I said.

"Oh." She sighed, looking genuinely disappointed. "I know it. Well, good for you—I wish I could quit something!"

"Really?" I looked at her. She practically glowed with health, confidence, and accomplishment. "Maybe you should."

She laughed and squinched her eyes a little at me in a really cute way. "Yeah, maybe. It would be fun to just hang out sometime."

"Everybody needs to hang out sometimes," Roxie said, dumping her bag of crap all over the floor in front of her locker, and then squatting down to sort through. "It's a medical fact."

"Maybe I'll have some people over this weekend," I suggested, much to my own surprise.

"Pool party!" Roxie yelled.

Susannah brightened even further. I dropped my new red sunglasses down to shield my eyes even though we were in the dim hallway.

"I'll give you my number," Susannah suggested tentatively. "If . . . I mean . . . whatever. We have that tournament in Scarsdale Saturday—oh, stress, we're gonna get whooped—but maybe after that? I was thinking of inviting some people over Saturday night, unless you—"

"No, yeah," I told her. "That sounds great." I handed my cell phone to the most popular girl in my grade and had her program in her phone number for me. It was surreal.

She left, calling over her shoulder, "See you later, Allison!"

It was the best day of school I'd had since the day in second grade when I lost my tooth *and* it was my birthday *and* my mom came to school with cupcakes and a book to read to my class *and* I got to say the morning announcements over the loudspeaker, all in one day. Back then I was actually friends with everybody, too—even Susannah Millstein. I was more fun in elementary school.

It hit me then that the girl I was kind of pretending to

be all day, as I hid behind my sunglasses, was like an older version of my elementary school self.

Okay, that is kind of a weird thing to be *pretending* to be, I realized. An older version of my younger self? What did I think I *actually* was, if not that?

That twisty thinking made me feel light-headed. I might even have been almost laughing to myself as I passed Jade, leaving school. She gave me one of her most killer looks. So apparently she still wasn't talking to me.

Oh, so what, I decided. Everybody else was, and Tyler Moss definitely kept finding ways to cross paths with me and say hey. I felt pretty confident that now he would call me, that I could have people over, that I was entering a new phase in my life, coming into my own, as my grandmother predicted I eventually would. I walked home swinging my arms, convinced for the first time in forever that it didn't matter one bit if Jade was pissed off.

I didn't find out how wrong I was about everything until I walked into my house.

16

MOM AND DAD WERE both sitting in the kitchen waiting when I got there.

"What?" I asked them.

Their arms were crossed over their chests and their faces were serious. I looked back and forth to try to figure out if they were sad or angry—if somebody had died, or if I had done something wrong. It was hard to tell.

"Did I do something?" I asked.

"Sit down," Mom said quietly. Angry. Yup. No question. I was toast.

"What did I do?"

"Sit. Down," Mom repeated.

I sat. The only words in my head were all curses. I waited. Nothing I said was going to hurry them or help me. I picked at my cuticles.

"Where did you go when you cut school Monday?" my father asked.

"Who said I cut school?" I asked, not denying it but still thinking I should know who told on me. That's a constitutional right, I reasoned.

"Did you?" Dad asked. Golly, they were both pale, even their lips.

"Let me assure you, Allison," Mom growled, "if you lie again now, you will be in even deeper trouble than you already are."

"How deep am I in?" I asked, wondering what she meant by *again*.

"Don't you be cute, miss," Mom barked, flattening me against my seat.

"I'm not." She was totally pissed. I was used to getting in trouble, but this was beyond. Her ears were pegged back on her head like an angry dog's. I had never seen her this mad, even at me.

"Where did you go?" Dad asked again, as patiently as if he were asking one of his balky kindergartners where she'd hidden the class gerbil.

"Into the city," I said, unsure how much to say, wondering how much they knew already. If Quinn had told on me, it would be probably about cutting school, though it could be about getting my picture taken too. But she wouldn't tell, not unless she was really worried. So that left Jade, who tells her mom way too much. If Jade's mom's nosiness won the internal battle with her appropriateness, she'd call my parents. In that case it would be about breaking my grounding

146

over the weekend, and then Mom or Dad would have said, *No, Allison wasn't grounded.* . . . That could explain the *again* comment about lying, maybe. So Jade was my number one suspect, I decided, possibly altering my career choice to detective, assuming I survived the afternoon.

"Where did you say you went?" Mom asked, meanwhile. She was no longer pale. *Uh-oh.*

"The city," I whispered again.

"Are you *kidding me*?"

Not sure if it was a real question or rhetorical, and not wanting to be cute, of all things, for the first time in my life, I started to shake my head, but then almost nodded, and then settled on a microshrug.

"With whom?" Dad asked.

"Roxie Green."

Mom shook her head. I could see she was making an effort to stay in her chair. I appreciated that. I was starting to get weirdly giddy. It was, horrifyingly, an effort to keep from giggling, which would have been nonsensical as well as suicidal.

"And what did you do there?"

"Nothing," I mumbled, keeping my jaw clenched.

"Nothing?" Mom repeated. "Nothing? Just wandered around the city? Like a couple of socialites with nothing to do?"

"No," I said.

"That's right, you didn't," Mom said. "I want to

hear from your own little lipsticked mouth what you did there."

That's when it hit me—somebody must have called from *zip*. Mom and Dad must know I went, and got my picture taken without their permission, maybe even that I forged Dad's signature.

"I-I can explain," I stuttered.

Mom and Dad sat there, their eyes intense and their bodies still. I took a breath, trying to find the beginning of my explanation.

That's when my phone went all-out in its unending attempt to screw up my life.

It buzzed with such intense vibrations I jumped off the chair, and then it was playing what sounded like traffic— horns beeping, tires screeching, metal crashing—all at top volume.

"Allison!" Dad said.

"I didn't . . ." I flipped open the phone. It was a 212 number, and the caller ID said ZIP. I closed the phone. The traffic noises resumed, so I pressed the Power button.

"Shut it off," Dad said sternly.

"I'm trying." I held it up to show that I was pressing the Power button as hard as I could, but the traffic jam in my palm continued.

"Allison, I will throw that phone in the garbage dis-posal, so help me," Mom yelled.

"I'm trying . . ." Nothing was working. Finally I opened

the phone, said, "Hello, I can't speak right now," and then hung up.

Silence. I pressed the Power button and the phone, like the most obedient of appliances, shut down instantly, and without a peep.

"Give me the phone," Mom demanded.

"I turned it off," I said.

"I don't care." Mom held out her hand, exactly the way the devil had. "Give me that phone."

I held it up to show her it was off and started saying, "It's off. I will tell you exactly what happened and I'm sorry, okay, I know . . ."

And then my phone started playing birdcalls.

Loudly.

Just as I was turning it to see who was calling me now, Mom grabbed it out of my hand, opened it up, and said, "Hello?"

She waited, fuming, then said, "Well, it's not going very well right now, Tyler Moss."

My mouth dropped open.

"No, I'm not Allison. I am her mother."

"Mom!"

"Yes, Tyler Moss, I will tell her that."

She closed my phone and put it down on the counter.

"Tyler Moss will see you in school tomorrow," she told me.

I let my head fall into my hands.

"You were about to tell us where you and your friend went instead of school on Monday, and why," my father prompted.

The buzzing inside my head was louder than anything my phone had yet invented. It was hard even to think.

"Allison," my dad said. "We're waiting."

"I know!" I said. They were both glaring at me. I took a few more breaths and tried to figure out how to explain. "Um, we went . . . It's just . . . we, well . . . See Roxie . . . Roxie's mom saw this . . . We just . . . The reason we went to—"

"Where?" Mom yelled, slamming her hand down on the counter. The slamming and yelling startled me so much I started to cry. The giggles I'd been squelching had flipped somewhere inside my chest and turned wet.

"Claire," Daddy said to Mom. "Let's stay calm. . . ."

"Stay calm? Are you kidding me, Jed? Stay calm? What should we do, just say, 'Oh, okay, Allison. That's fine. Did you have fun? What a great idea—just take the train into the city when we think you are at school and wander around without telling anybody and throw your life in the toilet. Great, honey.' Why? So we don't damage her fragile self-esteem?"

"Claire," Dad tried again.

"I want a detailed accounting," Mom growled at me. "You are already grounded for a month, little miss. And if you think we're letting you go to Tennis Europe, you're sadly—"

"You're not letting me go to Tennis Europe," I yelled back. "And it has nothing to do with whether I cut school or not. I'm not going to Tennis Europe because you screwed up at work and got yourself fired, big miss."

She picked up her hand like she was going to slap me, but I was too fast for her. I grabbed my phone and turned away.

Mom was fast, too. She grabbed my wrist and squeezed, hard.

"Drop that phone," she said, low and slow.

I dropped it.

"Talk," Mom said.

"We went into the city to go to a modeling tryout, for Roxie. I got my picture taken, too, because, well, otherwise I would have had to wait out on the street and I was scared to do that. Then we went to Starbucks, I got a doppio macchiato, she got a fribbiflabbichino something, and then we came home."

"Is that the truth?" Dad asked.

"Yes," I said.

"Go to your room," Mom said. "Daddy and I need to think about how to handle this. Right now we are too angry to discuss it further with you."

I swallowed hard and, relieved to be dismissed even

temporarily, reached for my phone to make a quick get-away.

Mom grabbed my wrist again. "Leave the phone, take the cannolis."

I looked up in her face. There was a slight possibility she was smiling, just with her eyes. Why was she paraphrasing *The Godfather* while still maintaining a death grip on my wrist?

When she let go, I grabbed my backpack and headed for the stairs. On the second step, I turned and asked, "When can I have my phone back?"

"We'll see," Dad said.

"I need it," I started to explain, until I caught a glimpse of my mother's jaw jutting forward and her eyes bulging out at me and changed my mind. Instead I took three steps at a time and didn't slow down until I was pressing my back against the door in my room.

17

WHEN I HEARD A QUIET knock on my door about an hour later, I had a fleeting thought that maybe it was Mom, and that she'd come in and we'd sit on my bed together and chat the way Jade and her mom always did, every night, and probably Roxie and her mom did, too.

"Go away," I said, not wanting to seem overeager.

"Let me in," said a slow, whispery voice on the other side. Quinn. Oh. I got up and let her in, then went and flopped down on my bed. I didn't even care that I was messing up all my neatly arranged white pillows.

"What happened?" Quinn asked, lying down next to me.

I dropped my arm over my eyes and told her the whole story. As always, she just listened quietly. After I finished, I waited for her to tell me what a jerk I was, how dangerous it was to cut school and go into the city, what a mess I had made of everything, what a terrible daughter and person I was. What could I even say to argue? I agreed. I was a total waste case. Not that that would have kept me from arguing; it just made me hate myself more.

But Quinn didn't say anything about that, or anything at all.

Great, I was thinking. I pour out my life trauma and it bores my sister so much she falls asleep? I gave it another few seconds and then peeked. She wasn't sleeping, so I didn't have to kill her. She was just lying there, blinking in her slow way.

"What?" I asked her, and then, since she wasn't showing any initiative in the let's-bust-Allison's-chops department, prompted her with, "So I guess I deserve it, being grounded, but what am I supposed to do about my cell phone?"

"I think—" Quinn started.

"Therefore you are?" I guessed.

"I think an English muffin is a happy day."

"What?"

She sat up and sang in her warbly voice, "An English muffin is a happy day, a happy day, a happy day."

Then I remembered. It was from a show she and I had made up in the bathtub at our old house, when we were little. We used to put tons of shampoo on our hair and then stand up in the bath, singing at ourselves naked and sudsily coiffed in the mirror, doing the Quinn and Allison Show. And one of our best numbers was "An English

Muffin Is a Happy Day."

So there we were in my big bed, both of us big, and dry, and dressed, and we started singing that wacky old song at possibly the worst moment of my life. From "An English Muffin Is a Happy Day," we moved quickly through our other great hits, like "Constipation: Lack of Doody-ation" and "Who Gassed?"

We were like eight-year-olds again, standing up, dancing on my bed, jumping around singing into our fists.

Eventually we wore ourselves out and flopped back down on my bed. "Well, that solved everything," I said after a few minutes.

"Good," she said. "Thought it might." She got up to leave. On her way out, she stopped and turned around. "I didn't tell on you."

"I think it was Jade," I said.

"She's worried about you," Quinn said.

"I know."

"Should she be?"

I shrugged. "Hard to say. Do I seem out of control to you?"

"No," Quinn said. "You just seem . . . kind of . . . happy, actually."

"Yeah, sometimes," I agreed. "Weird, huh?"

She shrugged. "You can use my cell phone if you need it."

"That's not the point!"

"I know, I'm just saying." She left, adding, "You're welcome."

"Thanks," I mumbled, but I doubt she heard.

A little later I went by Mom and Dad's room and sort of lurked in the doorway for a while, until Mom looked up from her desk, where my phone was sitting near her pile of papers.

"I actually really need my phone," I said.

"You actually really can't have it right now," she answered. "I'm not sure you understand how serious it is to cut school and just wander around the city, with nobody knowing where you are."

I almost argued that Quinn knew where I was, but stopped myself before implicating her. Instead, I said, "I do know. I said I was sorry."

She nodded. "I want to hear more about this thing you did, getting your picture taken—what the hell was that all about?"

"It was for a contest. Who's the most gorgeous teen today, or something."

"The most . . . what?"

"Gorgeous," I said.

"And you thought you . . . Ugh. We need to talk about this, but I have to finish this thing right now and get it to the lawyer before five." She checked her watch, cursed, then mumbled, "Most gorgeous teen, of all . . . ," and turned back to her work.

"I really need my phone," I said.

"You can use the landline," she said without looking up.

"I don't even know the numbers," I told her.

She groaned and turned around. "And who's Tyler Moss?"

"A boy."

"I gathered," she said. "Are you going out with him?"

"Am I not allowed to go out with somebody?"

"That's not what I said, Allison. I was just asking."

"No," I told her. "I'm not *going out* with him."

"Just . . . interested in each other?"

This was torture. This should be outlawed by the UN. "I guess."

"That's why you need your phone back?"

"No!" Why did she have to be so impossible? "Yes, him. But also Jade, Roxie, other people. If you want to punish me, fine. Do whatever you want to me; I don't care. But I have a life, you know, and I'm connected to it by my phone!"

"I don't like your tone of voice, young lady," Mom said to me.

"Well, it's mutual!" I yelled.

"Go to your room," she said, and turned back to her work again, dismissing me. I kicked her door as I left.

I had a bit of a tantrum in my room and then didn't clean up afterward. (So there! Not that anybody would care but me, and it was driving me nuts, but I left it a mess on principle.) When they made me go down for dinner, I did, but I didn't talk to anybody, just ate my dinner and cleared my plate. I went back up to my room and didn't budge from in front of my computer, even when I heard my phone doing its own little version of the Grammy Awards down the hall on Mom's desk. Phoebe knocked on my door a couple of times but I just couldn't deal with her.

It took a while, but finally Roxie got online so we could chat. As expected, she'd been trying to text me. I told her what had happened and realized only when she seemed confused that she thought my parents had already found out about our big day in the city by a call from the school, and were cool with it.

Why didn't u tell me the truth? she asked.

IDK, I responded. *I should have. Felt like a loser, I guess.*

U can tell me anything, u know that! Well, so that sucks. A month? She was as fast as I was: type, send, a good fast rhythm.

Yup, I whipped back.

Kiss up. Maybe they'll get past it.

Doubt it, I sent back.

How'd they find out, then?

Jade, I think.

Jealous bitch, she wrote instantly.

I laughed out loud, then typed, *Jealous? Of what?*

Well, of me, for one thing.

Maybe.

Also of you, Roxie shot back.

Why wd she be jealous of me? Why wd anybody be jealous of ME?

It took maybe ten seconds to get her response: *Because you aren't following her around all tense anymore like you have been all year. Because you hooked up with Tyler Moss. Because you look great, now that you're not hiding under your hair so much and always frowning. Lots of reasons.*

You're just saying that, I wrote back.

Just typing that. Not!

Before I could even respond, she sent:

How long r they keeping ur phone?

IDK, I typed. *R u gonna go 2 Susannah's party?*

Not w/o u! Do u need Tyler's # to call him back?

Yes! I typed back. *Thanks!*

No prob—getting it.

What do u think he was calling me about?

How hot u r, she replied.

Hahaha, I typed.

After she gave me his number, I typed,

Thanks. Not sure if I shd call him . . .

Hmmm, true, maybe make him wait a bit.

Yeah, I agreed. *But what about the woman from* zip?

I pressed Send before it hit me.

Shit.

I hit Delete but it was too late.

I hit Delete ten more times, even knowing it wouldn't help.

All I could do was wait, and then up came her response:

What woman from zip*?*

So there it was, choice time. What to do? I could try innocent: *huh?* Or muddleheaded: *Did I say* zip*? I meant the trip, Tennis Europe, who called. Earlier.* I could go with distraction: *Gotta go, my house just caught fire.* Or half-truths: *Some woman from* zip *called—I think I left my wallet when we went there.*

I decided on half-truth, and had actually typed it but stopped with my pointer in midair before hitting Send. I deleted it and started over:

Please don't hate me. I somehow got a callback. I don't know why. Maybe I got the joke spot. I didn't want to tell you because, well, this is what you wanted, not me—I was just along for the ride and now I feel like I accidentally stole your spot. Not that I could. I am a jerk. I'm sorry.

I reread it three times, hovered over Send, and then just sent it.

For about three hours (okay, maybe it was more like three minutes, but I swear I could feel myself aging) I sat and stared at my unmoving computer screen through my fingers.

Finally, her response flashed up:

Congratulations.

That was all. I quickly typed:

Are u mad?

GTG, she typed back. *More l8r.*

And then she signed out.

I sat in front of my computer for a few hours and, when I started twisting into a cramp, lay down on my bed, still watching the unchanging screen, cursing myself, wishing I could go back and redo everything.

Eventually I apparently fell asleep, because I woke up in the dark, still dressed, tangled in the stuff on my bed, and saw the devil sitting languidly on my couch, waiting for me to focus. He was wearing a beautiful gray suit and a crisp white shirt, open at the collar, and looked utterly at ease.

"Rough night?" he asked.

"No," I said, squinting. "Yes."

"That's what I like," he said. "Contrary, but absolute."

I rubbed the heel of my right hand hard against my eyes. "It's all your fault, isn't it?"

"What is?"

"You're totally messing with my phone—making it ring at crazy times and not putting my messages through, forcing my parents to take it away from me . . ."

"Why would I do that?"

I thought for a second. "Perversity?"

He smiled. "My favorite word."

"Mine too," I admitted. "You know it's totally screwing up my entire life, right?"

"Is it?" he asked.

"Yes," I said. "And not to put too fine a point on it, but you promised I would be gorgeous in return. Remember?"

"And you are."

"No," I said. That's when I noticed he was flipping through the issue of *zip* I'd had tucked under my mattress. "That doesn't count."

He cocked his head at me. "You don't think being chosen by the top new magazine, and my personal favorite, as one of the most gorgeous teens of the year counts?"

"So it was because of you," I said.

"You were chosen because they thought you were gorgeous," he argued softly, still flipping pages.

"Yeah, right."

"It's true."

"What are you doing here?" I asked him.

"Just visiting," he said, closing the magazine and smiling benignly with his lips closed. "As they say at the jail in Monopoly."

"What?" I asked.

He squinted his green eyes slightly. "Tyler Moss, hmm?"

"What about him?"

"Interesting," said the devil.

I sat up and crossed my legs. "In what way is Tyler Moss interesting?"

"Trust me," he said.

I laughed. "Oh, great advice. Trust you?"

He laughed, too, and said, "Touché."

We just sat there for a while not talking. It didn't occur to me to ask him if he was real or if I was dreaming, not until the next day. I was thinking instead about Roxie, and Jade, and my parents—how everybody was disappointed in me. How I had screwed everything up. What I really needed right then was somebody whose advice I could trust. And what I had instead was the devil, sitting on my couch.

Why was he really there? I started wondering, and then it hit me. This was it, end of the line. Our deal was completed. I got to be seen as gorgeous by seven people—I tried counting them up in my head—and now that my life was in the toilet because of his stupid games with my phone, and all my relationships (which had admittedly never been so great to begin with) were wrecked because of it, he was done. The fun was finished.

So I'd be ugly again by morning.

Yeah? Screw him.

"You're not just visiting," I said, as Mom-like as I could, tough and icy. I should have known it would never last. I did know, had known all along. Was he expecting me to fight? Cry? No way.

"Why do you think I'm here, then?" he asked, cool as ever.

"To turn me back into a pumpkin? It must be past midnight. You got sick of playing with my ring tones. That's it, right? You came to break the deal?"

He placed the magazine on my couch and stretched his long legs out in front of him. "I never break my deals," he said.

"Oh. Point of honor?"

"If you wish," he said.

"Because by my count, it's not seven, or even six if I traded one. Roxie, maybe Tyler but I'm not sure, maybe that woman from *zip*, who else? Are you counting Susannah Millstein? Or those big gorillas from the party? Because I don't think those people count. If those are the six, fine, but I think I could be justified in asking for a recount."

"Is that what *you* want, Allison?" he asked, all calm in contrast to me. "To end our little bargain? Were you hoping I came to return your phone to you?"

"Can I have it?" I asked, untangling my fingers from my hair and unclenching my face. "You can get my parents to give it back?"

He arched one eyebrow.

"Or did you mean the other kind of I could have it back?"

"Is that what you want, Allison?" he asked.

I thought about it. Did I? If I actually could go back, would I want to?

"It's up to you," he said.

"Seriously?"

"Seriously," he said.

I scratched my knotted hair and tried to think, but found I couldn't. "What do you think I should do?" I asked him. He was the only one there. Who else could I turn to?

"Not everybody has your best interests at heart," he said. "Hard to tell who's who, isn't it?"

I nodded.

"So unless you're sure, you'll have to trust your own judgment."

"Oh, great," I said. "I'm the last one I'd trust. Let me ask you this, then. Just between us—is there any chance I could actually, you know, be chosen?"

"There is always a chance, until you take yourself out of the running."

"Okay," I said.

"Okay," he said back. "We'll leave it at that, then."

"I don't break my deals, either," I said.

He had strolled over to my door. "Perversity, indeed," he said, his lips curling into a smile as he left.

18

I WOKE UP AGAIN WITH Quinn banging on my door. "I'm leaving in three minutes," she warned.

I looked at the clock and cursed. She couldn't have woken me up fifteen minutes earlier? I had to rip off my clothes, pull on new ones, and brush my teeth all at the same time. I just left my room a wreck, for the first time ever. I didn't even care.

Roxie wasn't on the bus. Jade slid in next to me when she got on.

"We need to talk," she whispered.

"Fine," I said, hiding behind my hair. "Talk."

She took a deep breath. "This is not about Ty, just so you know. I don't even like him."

"Okay," I said.

"I like David Kornhaber," she said. "He asked me out yesterday and I said yes."

"Congratulations."

"Are you going out with Ty?" she asked.

"No," I said, still looking out the window, but starting to feel a bit like a jerk, being so cold.

"But you like him."

"Yeah," I said.

"You make a cute couple."

I shook my head. Jade always surprised me. "Thanks."

"You're welcome. But, anyway, I'm really worried about you," she said quietly.

"Don't be," I answered.

"I'm your best friend," Jade whispered. "I love you, and I know you."

"Yeah?" I asked.

"Yeah," she said. "I do. And I know this is not you. You are nice, and reserved. You are neat and innocent and a little awkward maybe, but you are not like Roxie Green, all big and boastful and laughing out loud and strutting around like you love yourself."

I just sat there. She was right, of course. I had never walked around acting like I loved myself, not for years and years.

"If you want to dump me," Jade continued, and her voice cracked as she said, "that's okay. . . ."

"Jade," I said.

She was crying silently, big round tears streaking down her soft cheeks.

"Jade, come on," I said. "I don't want to dump you."
She sniffled.

"I don't."

"Roxie Green is gorgeous," she whispered. "And she's fun, I'm sure, more fun than I am, I guess."

"No, it's not that," I said, putting my arm around Jade, who rested her head on my shoulder.

"I'm sorry if I got you in more trouble," she said.

"Well, you did," I told her, secretly relieved to know she was the one who told and not Quinn. "But I'll survive."

"Good," Jade said. "Are we okay?"

"We're okay," I assured her. We got off the bus and walked into school together. She organized her stuff at her locker while I looked around for Roxie, and tried to think of what to say to her.

I finally saw her as Jade and I were heading in to first period, with Serena trying to squeeze between us.

"Hi, Roxie," I said.

"Hi," she answered, and went to her seat.

"Wow," Jade whispered in my ear. "What's wrong with her? Is she mad that you're talking with me?"

"No," I told her.

"Good," Jade said, and with Serena trailing after us, we headed into class. I spaced out through the entire thing, watching the clock.

In the hall afterward, Roxie grabbed me by my sleeve.

"Listen," she said. "I'm jealous as hell."

"Okay," I said.

"And you should have just told me. What's with all the secrets? Is that like a thing in this town?"

"I don't know," I admitted.

"Maybe it's a culture I just don't get here," Roxie continued, her face angrier than I'd ever seen it before. "Like having gazebos. What the hell are those things for anyway? And mudrooms. A whole room for mud? And the squeaky voices you have to use when you say the word *cutest*. Is that it? Are there just gaps in my knowledge? Am I like a foreigner here, thinking I'm waving hello but actually, like, giving people the finger without realizing it? Are we all just supposed to hide behind our manicured hedges and lie to our friends in this polite pit of purgatory?"

"Yes," I yelled back. "Didn't you get the mailing from the chamber of commerce?"

"I must've forgotten to read it!" she shouted.

We stared at each other there in the hall without moving for a few seconds. Everybody else was watching us, too. When I saw her left dimple deepen, I started to smile. She did too, but then stopped.

"Congratulations, you little shit."

"Thank you," I said.

"Congratulations on what?" Serena asked.

"It's none of our business," Jade whispered to her, loud

169

enough for everybody to hear.

"Allison is a finalist to be on the cover of *zip*," Roxie announced.

Everybody, including me, stared at her.

"Is that true, Allison?" Jade asked.

"No," I said. "Semifinalist."

Then the bell rang. We were all late.

Everybody pretty much stared at me the rest of the morning, and so I was totally dreading lunch. I wanted to avoid lurking like a loser near either Jade's or Roxie's locker, since neither was talking to me, but I didn't know what to do with myself. I decided maybe I would go in search of my own locker, and headed toward the gym wing, where I ran into Tyler Moss and his friend Emmett.

"Allison?" Ty said.

"Hi," I said, keeping my head ducked because I could feel myself blushing at the thought that he'd think I was a total stalker. Also I had zero makeup on, and he had only liked me the two times I'd been careful to do myself up. Not to mention I had recently made out with him.

"You okay?" Ty asked.

"Fine! Oh, sorry about my mom picking up."

"That's okay," he said. "What happened?"

I shrugged. "I cut school with Roxie one day last week and they found out."

"Whoa," Emmett said. "My parents would beat my butt if I cut."

"What did they do to you?" Ty asked, dumping books into his locker.

"Talked my ear off," I said. "Took my cell phone away. And grounded me for a month."

The two of them looked at each other.

"What?" I asked.

"Nothing. I texted you last night," Tyler said.

"I didn't . . ."

"Yeah. Also, I was thinking of having people over this weekend."

I didn't know what to say. He didn't tell me what he had texted, and he didn't exactly invite me to his party or get-together or whatever, but it did seem like he was implying he would have, if I hadn't been grounded. Trying to think of something cool to say, I decided to peek in his locker and see if I could comment on any of his subjects. There was a screwdriver on the top shelf of his locker.

"You take carpentry, too?" I asked, weirdly loudly. As soon as it was out of my mouth—well, and then when I saw the baffled look on his and Emmett's faces—I wished I could retract it. Or at least turn down the volume on it. Since I couldn't, I got myself in further, saying, "In addition to plumbing?"

"What are you talking about?" Emmett asked.

Unable to speak with my foot so far in my mouth, I pointed at the screwdriver. They both looked up, but didn't spot anything. "Screwdriver," I finally managed.

They both looked again, and then Emmett smiled. "You know Ty's brother, Gideon?"

"No," I said, at the same time Ty said, "Shut up, Emmett."

"What?" Emmett said to Tyler. "It's sweet." Tyler's face was dead serious, but Emmett continued, "Ty is a master unscrewer, because—"

"Shut the hell up," Ty said.

"Okey dokey," I said, turning to go.

"It's just . . ." Ty said. "Nothing against you. Just . . . family stuff is private, to me."

"I understand," I said.

"Thanks," he said back.

"Ask her," Emmett mumbled.

"Shut up," Ty grunted back.

Okay, if I had been blushing before, I must have been bright red by then. There was so much blood in my face, my feet were at risk of falling off. "What?" I asked, silently praying this was about to be the first time I was asked out—and that if it was, I wouldn't do something horrid like faint.

"Nothing," Ty said. "Where you headed?"

I tightened my backpack straps. "Looking for my locker."

"What do you mean?"

"Long story," I said.

Ty smiled, his crooked wise-guy smile. "Okay. We

heard this rumor . . . Are you, like, a model?"

"No!"

"I told you," Ty told Emmett.

"That's what everybody was saying," Emmett argued. "All morning. 'You know Allison Avery? She's, like, this big model, on the cover of a magazine; can you believe it?'"

"Rumors," I managed, but couldn't continue. The obviousness of how ridiculous the idea of me as a model seemed to them was too awful.

"Never mind," Ty said to me, and grabbed Emmett, punched him lightly a few times, and headed out the side door.

The corridor was so empty as I walked around the gym wing, my footsteps echoed. All of the locks looked identical, and equally familiar.

I tried a few at random, using combinations of my birthday, but nothing opened for me. I wandered down to the cafeteria feeling like a complete and total loser, and sat there eating my lunch and pretending to study my science textbook.

All afternoon, people stared as I approached and whispered as I passed. Jade, Serena, and Roxie continued to ignore me, but in a nauseatingly polite way. It seemed to be a nice bonding experience for the three of them. I even saw Jade whisper something to Roxie after sixth. I just wanted to die. It was the slowest school day ever.

And then when I got home, Phoebe was waiting there

for me, to spill out her troubles—something about the boy she liked liking her. It made no sense; it was just like bragging, but with a complaining voice. I almost had to smack her in the head, but I would've had to touch her shiny-straight blond hair, and that would just have been too much. She followed me to my room and made a snarky comment about how it was a mess and what was wrong, because it finally dawned on her that maybe she wasn't the only person in the world with stress, that maybe people were coping with things even worse than the boy you liked liking you.

I slammed her out and flopped down on my messy bed to throw myself a private pity party. Down the hall, I could hear my phone playing a sad little tune.

19

Mom came into my room a little later and sat down on my bed. I tried to wait her out, let her tell me why she was there, but eventually I couldn't stand it anymore, so I asked, "What did I do now?"

Mom took a deep breath and held my phone out in her palm.

"I can have it back?"

"The thing is possessed," she said.

"You have no idea." I scooped it out of her palm and gripped it in my own. It was heavier than I remembered it being.

"It won't stop chirping and burping and blaring out dance beats, all night long. How many gazillion friends do you have, calling at all hours?"

"Zero gazillion," I mumbled. "Zero."

"Well, they sure call you a lot, Allison, for a bunch of zeros."

We lay there against my pillows for a while, not talking.

"Doppio macchiato, huh?"

"Never again," I said.

Mom laughed, then sighed. "So you got your picture taken at a modeling thing?" she asked.

"Yeah," I said. "It was really weird."

"I bet!" she said. "You didn't . . . They didn't ask you to take your clothes off or anything, did they?"

"No!" I was picturing myself dropping my sweatshirt on the floor, but I knew that wasn't what she was worrying about. "No, it was just, like, three seconds. Smile! Faster than when Daddy takes our picture on vacation."

"Oh," Mom said. "And it was an audition?"

"Kind of."

"What were you auditioning for?"

"Really it was Roxie Green who was auditioning. I was just along for company, I guess. But, like, a cover feature on 'the New Teen' or some such crap."

Mom laughed. "You know what I love about you?"

"No," I admitted.

"You see through all the b.s. other girls would totally fall for. The New Teen. What a crock! And they yank in what, five hundred girls?"

"Over a thousand."

"Jeez. And how many even have the slightest chance of being 'the New Teen'?"

"Twenty," I whispered.

"Exactly. It's just cruel. Just a publicity stunt, probably, marketing subscriptions to these poor teenagers who never had the slightest chance."

It had never even occurred to her that I could be one of the twenty. She was off on a corporate tangent. I lay forgotten beside her on the bed.

"And so stupid!" she continued. "What kind of aspiration is that, anyway, to be a model? What, to be a clothes hanger? Ridiculous. I never understood the appeal."

"You can make a boatload of money," I argued pointlessly.

"You can make more money other ways," she said, sitting up, getting way into this. "On average it's probably more cost-effective to work at Starbucks. But how many girls would do anything to be a model?"

"Lots," I said, draping my arm over my face.

"Exactly. And why?"

"To be seen," I mumbled.

"Exactly," she said. "To be looked at. It's as if they don't exist if they aren't famous or something. So sad. But you—you just see right through the hype, the false promise of fame, glamour, beauty, don't you?"

"Me? Sure," I said. "Right on through it."

"How many girls are flopped across their beds crying and hating themselves because they can never measure up to the impossible standards of beauty held out in those crappy magazines?"

"Uncountable numbers of us," I said.

Mom laughed again and said, "You are wicked."

"Probably," I said.

She sighed. We had run out of stuff to bond over, now that we were done trashing the only thing I'd ever gotten chosen for.

"How's the lawsuit going?" I eventually asked her.

She shrugged. "How's adolescence?"

"That bad?" I asked her.

"If memory serves," she said, "maybe even worse."

"Yeah, but for you that's not saying much," I said. "You were probably like Phoebe, all smooth and pretty and lucky in every way."

Mom chuckled. "No."

"Or like Quinn, brilliant, perfect, well behaved . . ."

"Grandma called me a lot of things when I was a teenager," Mom said. "But well behaved was not one of them."

I lowered my arm and turned to look at her. She was kind of smirking a little, but her eyes were sad.

"Fighting the world is not always easy," she said. "I always felt like I had to prove myself. I still do. You, too?"

I nodded.

"You're going to be a big success someday, Allison Wonderland. You mark my words."

I held my breath. I wanted to stop time, right there, before she got to the next part, which would probably be a criticism, or at least a qualification: *If you would just stop screwing everything up; if you would just please not be so difficult; if you could manage to be more like Quinn.* But so far there it was, just *a success.* And she hadn't called me Allison Wonderland since I was a little kid, when I went through a brief easy period. *You're going to be a big success someday, Allison Wonderland.* This felt less real to me than negotiating with the devil. I held very still, balancing the words carefully above my head. I didn't want to do anything that would make me find out I'd been dreaming this time.

She stood up. "A big success," she repeated, as she covered the distance to my door in six long steps. "And when you do make it, when you succeed—and you will, Allison—I will be so proud of you."

She left, her words echoing in my head.

When I succeed, she will be proud of me.

I lay there for a while repeating that to myself, and then remembered I'd gotten my phone back. When I grabbed it and checked my messages, this is what I saw:

All 17 messages have been deleted.

Screw you, I texted back, but, with no number to send it to, deleted it and dropped the phone on my bed.

I took a shower, listening to the echo of my mother's words. I dried my hair, put on moisturizer, repeating to myself: *When I am successful, she will be proud of me.* I was staring at myself in the mirror, wondering if she was right that someday I could be a success, and what it would feel like for her to be proud of me, when I heard my phone beeping.

You have 1 new voice mail.

It was a message from the woman at *zip*, saying, "We are trying to reach Allison Avery. The message on this phone is cryptic. If this is the correct number, or if it is not, please call back and confirm that Allison Avery will be at our studio for a photo shoot next Monday at two p.m."

I stood there, dripping in my towel, trying to figure out what to do. *When you are a success, and you will be, I will be so proud of you. But not until then,* she didn't have to add.

Fine, then.

I would prove to her, to everybody, to Tyler and Emmett and Jade and everybody else at school, to Phoebe and Quinn, Grandma and Dad and especially to Mom—who's *interesting-looking* now? Maybe the ugly duckling isn't just ugly. Maybe the experts know more, and chose me. Out of all those poor deluded schlubs, they wanted me. Me.

I grabbed the phone and hit the Send button to dial them back. While it connected and started ringing, I was thinking how weird, that maybe in this horrible town where I never fit in because the one thing that matters at all is being gorgeous, the most gorgeous girl is me.

Me? Gorgeous?

It was too ridiculous to even say inside my own head, so as the woman's voice mail picked up, I thought about the ten thousand bucks. What would Mom say when I handed her the check? Would she cry? Hug me? Tell me she couldn't take it? Even if she refused, she'd have to be impressed with me, right?

You are a success, Allison Wonderland.

Yeah, except that first she'd have to ground me for the rest of my life for going to the callback. The voice mail message finished. *Beep!* They would totally kill me if I cut again and went into the city, and no way would they give me permission. I shut the phone and dropped it on my bed.

Still in my towel and shivering, I was also in a sweat. *Forget it,* I told myself. *I'm not the gorgeous type. It was fun and kind of funny. Now it's over.*

As I headed back to the bathroom to dry off, my phone buzzed again. I dashed back to it, sure the woman from *zip* had seen my number and caught me. What to do? But no, it was a new text, from Roxie:

U there yet?

My hands were shaking. *Yes,* I typed, and lamely added, :)

In three seconds my phone beeped, and I read her response:

Chamber of commerce?

I quickly texted back:

U still mad?

Almost done, though still WAY jealous, you gorgeous lunk. Any other secrets u'r hiding?

I started to answer no, but then thought about the fact

that my mother had gotten fired, our family finances were apparently in tatters, that I couldn't go to Tennis Europe because we couldn't afford it, and and and . . .

Yes, I texted back instead. *Many.*

Did Ty ask u out?

That, I wd've told u!

Emmett asked me out, she texted to me.

!!!! Did u say yes?

Yes. :)

Call me, I typed, my thumbs tripping over each other. *I want details!*

We talked for over an hour. The whole time, as she told me every detail of her conversation with Emmett on their walk home after school, I just kept thinking how lucky I was that she had (mostly) forgiven me.

"Anyway, I'm psyched for you," she insisted, turning back, unfortunately, to the subject of me. "Most auditions they don't choose you—so this time it wasn't me. You can't take it personally or you'd be pummeled into a pulp every day of your life."

"Maybe that's my problem," I told her. "I do take everything personally."

"Yeah, so that explains why you're kind of pulpy, I guess." She laughed, then stopped. "But seriously, why wouldn't you just tell me?" she asked.

I had no good answer other than "Um, because I am

a jerk? And because maybe I never had a generous friend before, so I don't know how to cope with it."

"Oh, Allison," she said. "Well, anyway, I really am so happy for you. Though maybe we could work toward less pulpiness?"

"Okay," I agreed. "Gets in your teeth, ew. Hate pulp."

Was she such a good person, I couldn't help wondering, or was it that she was so friendless and desperate that she still needed me even though she hated me? Then I hated myself for thinking such nasty, shallow stuff.

But the devil was right: Telling who has your best interests at heart is not an easy trick.

The next few days of school went much smoother—it was, like, weird to say, but, like, everybody liked me. People were kind of kissing up to me, even. Boys checked me out, and not in an *ew, what is with your hair* way, either. I admit, I was wearing T-shirts and shorts instead of big tennis team sweatshirts or either of the hoodies I'd gotten from people's bat mitzvahs the year before, the way I had been all year. I was brushing my hair every morning (I know, very impressive), and on Friday, I bobby-pinned the front off to the side. It looked a little funky, but the girl on the front of the new copy of *zip* had it like that, so I knew it wasn't a completely hideous thing to try, in theory anyway. Three girls, including Susannah Millstein, complimented me on it.

Jade was back to treating me like her best friend and being excited for me about Tyler Moss, though at lunch she and Serena were hanging in the Model UN room with David Kornhaber and that crowd. She invited me, but I made the excuse of needing air. I tensed for her reaction. She didn't slide her eyes away, disappointed; she said okay and grinned at me. Just another weirdly happy thing in a week stuffed full of easy smoothness. If I didn't bruise so easily I might've pinched myself.

Outside, since Roxie was walking around holding hands with Emmett, I got to spend some time with Tyler. I couldn't stop myself from asking him, repeatedly, about the screwdriver. He gave me a different wise-guy answer every time ("I have an after-school job as a bartender," "I'm in the screwdriver club"), but he didn't look annoyed, so I asked again. On Friday, he didn't smirk. He said, "You really want to know?"

"Yeah," I said. "I think I do, at least."

"My brother, Gideon? He's eleven. Yeah, well, he's got Down syndrome. You know what that is, right? He has mental retardation."

I nodded. He smelled like fresh air.

"So, anyway," he continued. "Gideon is not that great at a lot of stuff, like school or sports or anything. What he likes to do is tighten screws. So . . ."

"So?" I asked.

"So I loosen screws."

We were sitting on a bench near the far fence, and he was leaning his elbows on his knees, talking very quietly toward his sneakers, so I wasn't sure I was getting the whole thing. "You do what?"

"When I get home, you know, I go around and loosen screws on stuff—doorknobs, chairs, the TV remote—and he goes around checking." Ty shrugged. "It makes him happy. Anyway, Emmett found that little screwdriver in his mom's toolbox and brought it in for me. That's why it was in my locker."

We sat there for a while then, listening to the sounds of people talking, yelling for the ball, flirting, joking. He tilted his head and looked up at me sideways, and asked, "What?"

"That's the nicest thing I ever heard."

"Shut up," he said.

"I thought you were all wise-guy obnoxious."

"Sorry to disappoint you," he said.

"I'll get over it," I told him. "Your brother is so lucky to have you."

"No way," Ty said, suddenly serious, maybe even angry.

"Yes, he really is," I argued. "Can't you take a compliment? It's true."

"No," Ty said, and looked away. "Everybody says that. But it's not . . . Look, I'm not saying I suck; I'm okay. But what people don't get is that really I'm the lucky one."

"Well, sure, but—"

"That's not what I mean," Ty said. "I mean, sure, I

185

was born lucky; the parts all work. But I mean, you don't know Gideon. He, like . . . the kid loves me more than anyone ever will. It's amazing. Just, like, with no strings, no conditions. Just . . . completely."

"That must feel great."

"It does," Ty said, his smile tilting a corner of his mouth up. "Also, he lets me be generous. You know? How often in life do you get a chance to do something that makes somebody happy?"

I shrugged. "I don't, really . . ."

"I do, every day," Ty said. "All I have to do is unscrew a few screws, and I make the kid's day. He smiles at me and . . . Anyway."

"I get it," I whispered.

"Thanks."

We kind of stared at each other for a few seconds then, and I was thinking maybe he would try to kiss me right there on the bench and that if he did I would be into it even though I normally think PDAs are gross, and then I thought maybe he would ask me out, especially since his best friend and mine were walking toward us holding hands (I have good peripheral vision), but instead the bell rang and he stood up suddenly.

On the way back into school, Roxie asked, "Hey, Allison, when do you go back to *zip* for the next round?"

"I'm not going."

She stopped short and Emmett smashed into her.

"Are you frigging kidding me?" she demanded.

"Where aren't you going?" Ty asked me.

"She was chosen as a finalist—sorry, semifinalist—for a cover-girl contest for *zip* magazine—and she's blowing it off?"

"So you *are* a model!" Emmett said. "She said—"

"I'm *not* a model," I interrupted. "It was this weird thing, a mistake, and anyway I'm grounded, and it's not like I have any chance at winning . . ."

"Why not?" Tyler asked.

"Because . . . ," I said, but couldn't finish.

"Because what?" Roxie demanded, hands on hips. "You think this is no big deal? Don't you know there are girls who'd give, like, a nonvital organ to have this chance, and you're just so above it all you can't be bothered to go for a frigging photo shoot? Get over yourself, honey."

"Get over myself?"

"Yeah. You remember the quote from Golda Meir?"

"No," I said, putting my hands on my hips, too.

"That's because you were in the hall recovering during Orly Rothstein's project!"

"I'm sorry I missed it!"

"You should be!" Roxie barked back. "Because Golda Meir, she was, like, some famous woman in Israel or something, and very smart."

187

"Okay."

"Yeah, well, she said, 'Don't be humble; you're not that great.' "

I smiled. Then Roxie smiled.

"I can't tell if you guys are fighting or kidding," Emmett said.

"Me either," I admitted.

"You really blew them off?" Roxie asked me.

I nodded.

"We have to call them right now," she said. "Where is your cell phone?" She held out her hand.

I gave it to her.

The warning bell rang, but we all stayed still, in the hall, while people dashed around us, and Roxie scrolled through my calls until she apparently came up with *zip*. She pressed Send and waited.

"Yes, hello," she said, sounding adult and efficient. "This is Allison Avery calling to confirm my appointment? Yes. I'm sorry. It's been a crazy week. I understand. Yes. No, it won't happen again— When? Monday at two? Is there a later— Yes, I understand. No problem. I'll be there. Thank you."

She hung up and handed me my phone.

"Roxie," I started.

"We'll figure it out," she said, dashing off. "I have to get to Earth science—wa-hoo!"

Ty stared at me. "You still grounded?"

"Yeah."

He smirked, and then, as the bell rang, he loped down the hall toward the tenth-grade wing, yelling, "See ya."

So that was that, then, and I had nothing to look forward to except explaining to my bio teacher why I was late and then a weekend full of nothing except Phoebe's middle school graduation and panicking about Monday. Or so I thought.

20

WATCHING PHOEBE GIVE her speech at her middle school graduation, I felt like my heart was going to break for her. Which was weird, because normally I mostly wanted to shove her out a window. But there she was, looking all shiny and sweet as always, giving the speech because she was the president of the class (of course), and I was all set to scrunch down in my seat and mutter curses under my breath while she spun out some lame metaphor of how the graduating eighth grade was like a pot of stew or some such bull, but then there was an odd moment when she, like, freaked out and dropped the papers her speech was typed on and started crying and then, wham, out of nowhere, there was Phoebe telling her deepest feelings to the whole freaking auditorium. I missed a couple of her points when somebody's grandpa who couldn't hear through the hair in his ears kept shouting, "WHAT DID SHE SAY?", but I got most of it. She was going off about this dress she fell in love with, which was this supposedly amazing green Vera Wang that I had heard my parents arguing about (baby monitor), and how when she couldn't have it she felt like her life was practically over.

I was like, *How is my sister so spoiled?*

Her life was ruined by not getting a dress? A green dress? Please.

I rolled my eyes at Quinn, who leaned close and whispered, "You don't think she'll tell about Mom, do you?"

"No," I said, just because no is my default answer; then I started worrying. *No,* I agreed with myself then. *No way Phoebe confesses Mom's sins, or failures, whatever, to the whole damn town. No way.*

I sat up and listened carefully after that.

She didn't. Poor Phoebe, she stood up there crying, with her mascara running down her face, and told about how she had learned how to be a good friend, and how lucky she was to have all of us. I almost started to cry, too, and when she stopped for a few seconds, staring out at us like she was so lost and alone in the world, I almost ran up and grabbed her off the stage.

Afterwards, after the standing ovation and the hugs all around, I was feeling really terrific about myself. What an awesome sister I was, lecturing her to get her head out of her butt and realize other people had problems, when she had obviously been completely dumped by her friends and was feeling so alone, but all I could think about was my own crap. What an excellent person I am to throw the first stone.

So when Quinn was telling Phoebe on the car ride home that maybe she could have compared the green dress in her speech to the green light Jay Gatsby looks at across the water in F. Scott Fitzgerald's masterpiece, I finally had to tell Quinn to shut up and leave her alone, the speech was perfect as it was.

Phoebe looked appreciative, though still, honestly, pretty wrecked.

Her graduation party with her friends was that night, but she wasn't going. She was staying home like Cinderella without her dress. Which made me and Quinn the ugly stepsisters, I guess. I was telling that to Quinn and trying to move her past the fact that I had belittled her *Gatsby* reference when the doorbell rang.

Neither one of us was sure it was really the doorbell, because it wasn't the normal one. We both realized at the same second that it was the front doorbell, and raced down the stairs together, yelling, "Coming! Hold on!" Then, since neither of us could figure out how to open the front door (which nobody as far as I could remember had ever actually used), we yelled to whoever it was ringing again and again to go around to the side door.

Quinn and I ran through the kitchen and out the side door. A small woman was standing outside our double front doors, holding a garment bag from Neiman Marcus and pushing the doorbell. We shrugged at each other and went to find out what was up.

Well, apparently it was the green dress. Phoebe's best friend had bought it I guess, and sent her housekeeper over with it for Phoebe to wear to the graduation party that night. I had to get Phoebe out of the pool and into the shower to get ready and go out to the party in it.

So much for her life falling apart.

"Is she the luckiest person ever?" I asked Quinn as we collected shoes and makeup for her.

"Absolutely," Quinn said. "Always has been."

"You're mad about *Gatsby*."

"Be ignorant; I don't care," she said. And then, as we were doing Phoebe's hair, she accidentally/on purpose brought up the whole thing with *zip*. I didn't really mind. Phoebe looked shocked, but at least she said, "Good luck." Instead of, "Why would they choose you," or something. I did her eyes smoky. Everybody complimented her on them, and then Mom drove her off to the party.

I texted *Have fun* to Phoebe and then slumped down with Quinn in front of the TV in the family room, until my phone groaned.

"You have the most messed-up ring tones," Quinn said.

I thought it would be Phoebe calling back to say thanks, the polite freak, but it was Jade. "How was Phoebe's graduation?" she asked.

"Okay," I said. "She gave the speech." I shrugged at Quinn.

"I know," Jade said. "Someone said she messed up?"

"Who said?" I asked. A commercial came on for Home Depot, and a guy was holding a screwdriver.

"Do you want to watch this or not?" Quinn asked.

"It's Jade," I whispered. "People are dumping on Phoebe's speech."

"She was great," Quinn said. "Who said what?"

"Maybe I misheard," Jade said at the same time, smooth and sweet. "I hope so. It was good?"

"She was great," I said again, watching Mr. Screwdriver build shelves for his curly-haired son's room on TV. "She rocked. Who said she messed up?"

"Why are you getting so Mafia about it?" Jade asked.

"She's my sister."

"Since when?"

"Since she was born."

"Can you hang up?" Quinn asked. "It's on."

"I meant," Jade snarled, "since when do you care about that?"

She had a point, but I just said, "Leave it. Okay?"

"Fine," Jade said.

"Sorry. I just—"

"Tell her I said congratulations."

"I will. Thanks, Jade."

"I'm gonna go take a shower," Quinn said.

"No, stay with me," I called after her, but she left.

"Roxie said you're going to the callbacks Monday?" Jade said. "For your modeling thing?"

"I—I don't know. I guess." I had to pace, so I went to the kitchen. Anyway, it was no fun to watch stupid reruns alone. "Weird, huh?" I said to Jade. "Me, modeling?"

"Now that you mention it, yes," Jade said. "I mean, not that you're not pretty. Just . . . I mean, you're so smart and real, I didn't think you'd be interested."

"Neither did I."

"But I think it's great. You know I've got your back, completely, whatever you do. Right?"

"Right," I said.

"It's weird, though. Roxie seems to have some mixed feelings about your success, huh?"

"Well," I said. "Not really."

"I just meant the whole yelling-in-the-hall thing, plus—"

"She was mad I didn't tell her, is all."

"You think so?"

"Totally," I said. "You should get to know her, Jade. She's not what you think. Well, you talked to her a bit this week. Right? She's not, like, wild and nasty; she's sweet!"

Jade just sort of hummed, "Mmmm."

"Seriously," I continued, all of a sudden feeling a manic need to convince Jade of Roxie's coolness, thinking I could somehow bring everybody together and life would be great. "Like, I wasn't even planning to go on the call-back for the *zip* thing? But Roxie called them up and made the appointment for me for Monday!"

Silence, then, "Did she?"

"Yes."

"Okay, Allison? I have to ask you something."

"Okay," I said.

"Why do you think she would do that?"

My hands were starting to shake, like they had after the doppio macchiato. "Because she's a good friend."

"Suddenly?" Jade asked. "She's suddenly your best friend?"

"No. She's just . . . She's nice," I said feebly.

"Think, Allison. Why would Roxie set you up, force you to go to this modeling shoot when you don't even want to, and it's what she wants more than anything?"

I opened the fridge and looked in. "Because she . . ."

"Come on, I don't want to hurt your feelings, but really, Allison. Let's be realistic—are you really the model type? I mean, to me you're a very nice-looking girl, and I love you to death, but really, do you honestly think you've got the stunning, magnificent looks of a model?"

"No," I admitted, and closed the door.

"Allison," Jade whispered, "I like her. She's fun, and funny. I have no problem hanging out with her sometimes. But this stinks. She's setting you up. It's cruel. I don't mean to be harsh—I just don't want to see you get hurt."

"But . . ." I sat down on the floor. Jade was right. Who did I think I was? Awkward, invisible, unattractive me, and then suddenly I have a weird dream and I turn magically gorgeous? It didn't make any sense. I had just been fooling myself. How completely embarrassing to be such a gullible fool.

"Allison?"

"Yeah," I said.

"Hi!" Jade said.

"I'm here. I'm just—"

"That is the *cutest* skirt!" she said.

I looked down at my fold-over-top leggings and sweat-shirt and asked, "What?"

Jade gave a quick laugh and said, "I know, I know! Can you believe it? No, be in in a sec. My mom, you know."

"Jade?" I asked. "Where are you?"

"At the party," she whispered. "The one on Maple. You know, everybody . . ."

"Oh." I hauled my fat ass off the floor. "Yeah, me too."

"Really?" she asked. "You're here? I thought you were still grounded."

"I thought you hated me." I opened the fridge and looked for something.

"I love you; you know that," Jade purred. "You're my best friend. That's why I'm calling. Wait, let me make sure nobody . . . Hey! Thanks."

"What?" I pulled out a smoothie bottle and read the back. Holy calorie count.

"I'm hanging up," she whispered. "I'll text you. It's safer."

I hung up and prayed my phone would stay normal for once. Screw calories; I wasn't going to be thin for Monday anyway, if I did go. I twisted off the cap and was halfway through chugging the smoothie when Jade's text came through:

Well, I wanted to warn you, and this is part of why I was saying watch out—I think Roxie Green is after Ty.

No way, I texted back. *Jk???*

No. :(They r getting way cozy on the couch. Serena thot I shdnt tell u but I knew u wd want 2 know. I hope I was right to.

This was bigger than a smoothie could soothe. For this I needed to call in both Ben and Jerry. I closed the freezer so I could sit against it, took a big spoonful, and texted, *cozy?*

Very.

But she's going out with Emmett, I texted, and then dug in my spoon for another cold hunk of comfort.

Apparently not anymore.

What r they doing?

It's gross. I thought she was ur friend.

I ate a few more globs of ice cream and then texted back, *I don't care.*

I wished that were true. *Damn.* The one good friend I'd

ever thought I had, the one boy who ever actually seemed to like me. I hated everyone right then, but most of all my wishful, gullible self.

Y wd they do that to u? Jade texted. *Do u think Roxie is jealous bc zip chose u instead of her?*

IDK, I texted. *Do u?*

Her text came through in a second: *Yes. I do.*

Roxie Green is a jealous slut, I texted back.

And then my phone completely died.

21

THE REST OF THE WEEKEND was hell.

Sunday morning Quinn woke me up to sneak back to the guest room to spy again because Mom and Dad were in the study. When we got the baby monitor working, we heard them talking about whether they were going to lose the house. *How do you lose a house?* I almost asked, but then I got it: lose, like not own it anymore. Our house? Quinn and I stared at each other with our hands over our mouths. "Did she say she cashed out her equity as collateral?"

I shrugged. "Some of those words, I guess. You know what that means?"

Quinn closed her eyes. "It means we're going to lose everything."

I put my arms around her and we just sat like that for a while.

Compared to that, really, my friendship problems were

nothing. That's what I told myself. The thing was, that didn't cheer me up at all. It's not like, *Oh, now it's all in perspective*; more like, *Oh, great, absolutely everything sucks at once.* It just felt like the floor was turning to dust under me and there was nothing solid to grab on to.

My phone, despite being plugged in, read, *Unable to charge*. Sometimes, just to taunt me, it beeped twice and flashed the words in green, blue, yellow, red: *Unable to charge*.

Nobody was online, either.

Phoebe, golden child, woke up just before noon and told us over cereal what a great time she'd had at her party. Even in my crabby state I managed to be a little happy for her, despite the fact that Mom had lent her the necklace she never took off, and Phoebe kept pawing the sapphire hanging there in her tan little neck notch. *We see it,* I managed to not scream. I just complimented her on how she looked, listened to what a great time she had with her friends and also kissing her boyfriend at the end in the parking lot under a weeping willow—and managed not to throw up even once.

Quinn and I decided not to tell Phoebe yet about the house. At least we could protect her for a little while. We told ourselves we were being good sisters to her.

I went to bed feeling so darned proud of myself. Not. I lay there going over my situation. My family was screwed.

We were going to have to move—out of our house, my house, my home. And to where? With no money, where were we expecting to go? Maybe we would have to move in with my grandmother. *Holy crap.* Just as I was finally drifting off into a nightmare, my phone honked twice, to remind me that it was unable to charge. *Thanks, great.* And my life was unable to claw its way out of the toilet. I decided to stop obsessing about family and torture myself about friends instead: My old ex–best friend was probably giving me the silent treatment for (she had to think) blowing her off mid-texting, which, to Jade, would be the height and depth of bitchiness. She was ignoring me online, anyway, and wouldn't answer her cell when I called from the landline. My new ex–best friend was apparently lying when she said she forgave me for lying to her (I know, I know, karma is a boomerang) and as revenge was hooking up with the boy I loved. Who was, of course, more into her. Who wouldn't be?

And I had an appointment to try to be a model smack in the middle of English, in twelve hours. During the final I hadn't studied for. Great, maybe I could add failing out of high school to my list of glorious accomplishments. That was when I remembered my other homework from English that I'd blown off completely because it was too ridiculous to even attempt: write your autobiography in six words. Yeah, right. How about, *I need more than six words*?

I got a pen and wrote that down, just in case we had

to read our autobiographies out loud. That got me thinking that maybe I would go for the photo shoot, if only to avoid the horror show of trying to write essays on books I'd never read.

Sleep was obviously out of the question, so I went to the bathroom. When I flicked on the light, the quote card Jade had made was the first thing I saw, and as I wondered if I had done anything all day that scared me, I caught a glimpse of myself in the mirror and jumped. Okay, seeing yourself in the mirror might not have been what Mrs. Roosevelt meant, but I was kind of a sight.

My eyes were bugging out with intensity, and my hair was practically standing straight out in all directions.

Gorgeous? Ha!

I took a good close look at my face, trying to see for real if anything had changed other than my phone's personality. It was hard to tell, because I generally tried to avoid looking too closely and therefore often didn't recognize myself in mirrors. My eyes, with their hard-to-say-what color, were still way far apart from each other. My nose was still long and narrow, with a slight detour halfway down. My lips had disappearing issues, and that hideous mole still camped out near my mouth. Nope. It was just a dream, a fluke, a nothing. *I would be an idiot,* I told myself, *to even think I have a shot.*

And why would I even care? It's not like all my life I'd wanted to be a model. I was so not about my looks—I couldn't be farther from a pretty girl, hot and cute and sexy. Oh, please! I totally never cared how I looked or what I wore. I mean, sure, it would be nice, I thought, to have people think I was hot. Or even cute. But that wasn't me. I was more of a . . .

I stopped, my hands resting on either side of my sink, and stared into my eyes in the mirror.

I am . . . what? In six words . . .

I am Quinn's sister and Phoebe's.

I am not a gorgeous girl.

I am getting my homework done!

Insecure lonely insomniac, taking life bumpily.

Despite complete self-absorption, unrecognizable in mirrors.

I picked up my brush and tried to yank it through my ratty, crazy hair, but there were just too many knots and it was making my eyes water. I threw open the under-sink cabinet and grabbed the scissors.

Stop, I told myself. *This is always, always a mistake.*

So the hell what? I decided, and started to cut my hair off.

"What did you do?" Phoebe asked me in the morning when I came out of my room, dropping my dead cell phone into my backpack anyway, for luck.

"Bad?" I asked, touching my choppy short hair.

Her big green eyes opened wide as she tilted her head

and looked at my hair. "Different," she said. "Maybe you need gel."

"Okay," I said, and followed her to her bathroom.

As she wet her hands and rubbed some gel between them, she asked if anybody else had seen my new style yet. I told her she was the first. She smiled, then stood back to look at my gelled hair. She started to laugh, and wouldn't let me look in her mirror.

"Phoebe!" I yelled.

"I'll fix it, I'll fix it," she said.

"I'm gonna miss the bus," I complained. "Why are you still in your pajamas?"

"I'm done," she said. "Remember? I'm in high school now! I'm so psyched."

"Oh, you should be," I said. "It's a total party."

"You want some lip gloss?" she offered.

I turned and checked myself out in the mirror. I looked like a stranger. "No, thanks," I said.

"I didn't really understand your text that you sent me at my party."

"There wasn't anything to get," I told her. How does she manage to walk around that bubbleheaded? How confusing is *have fun*?

She shrugged. "Okay. How about my long socks?" I tried to stop her but she ran into her room and yanked stuff out of her already overflowing drawers until she came up with the longest pair of tube socks I'd ever seen.

"Why, did you wreck my flip-flops?"

"No," she said. "You just look so funky with the hair, I thought . . ."

I took her socks and tugged them on. She stood back and looked. "Cool," she said.

"As cool as the other side of the pillow?" I asked.

She laughed. It was a really sweet, generous laugh. "Sure. Yeah. Definitely cool. Wear your Chucks."

"You think?" I checked her full-length mirror and, with my red sunglasses dropped down over my eyes to prevent me from making eye contact with myself, I almost kind of agreed.

"You should go," she said.

I cursed and dashed out, but at her door I stopped and said, "Thanks. Hey, Phoebe?"

"Yeah?"

I tried to think of how to ask her advice about whether I should cut school to go into the city by myself and try to be a model, or blow it off and lie low and not make a fool of myself and probably get in trouble again. But the answer was so obvious I didn't even have to ask.

"Congratulations," I said instead. "On graduating."

She smiled her radiant, perfect smile. "Thanks," she said. "Everybody is going to love how you look today," she called after me as I dashed down the stairs. "I swear!"

Well, *love* might have been a strong word. Everybody noticed, that was for sure. On our way to the bus, Quinn had stared, but eventually said no, it actually looked very cool, and asked if everything was okay with me. I told her everything was fine and couldn't a person cut her hair without it raising alarms? She left me alone after that.

A few people complimented me, including Susannah Millstein, who said, "You look great! What's up?"

"Nothing," I said.

"I got your text, and . . ."

I tried to think if I had texted her. I hadn't.

"I didn't see Roxie today," Susannah said, then leaned close and whispered, "Maybe she didn't want to face you."

"Were you at the party Saturday night?" I asked her.

Susannah blushed. "Well, not at the . . . Did you mean mine? I just had a few people over. Well, two people. So it wasn't, like, a party, not like the one everybody . . . So, I guess most people didn't really want to come to mine so much, but I didn't think ninth graders . . . I texted you about it, but you didn't . . . So, I just figured you were at the . . ."

"Sorry," I said. "I didn't get your text."

"No, no, mine was way boring anyway. No worries," Susannah said, and smiled weakly. "Plenty of chips left, if you want to come over sometime . . ."

"Sounds great," I said.

Jade walked by fast, ignoring me even when I called her name. I followed her to first period and slipped into my seat, feeling everyone's eyes on me.

"Allison?" the Fascist asked.

"What?" I asked defensively. Did she think I really cared what *she* thought about how I looked? *Could everybody just stop looking at me like that, please?*

She handed me a slip of paper. I'd apparently been chosen to present as Gouverneur Morris at the Wednesday assembly. "Congratulations," she said, beaming at me. "You did a good job. You've really pulled yourself together lately." Then she whispered, "And you look terrific, too. Good luck on the final!"

I cursed silently for having forgotten all about the social studies final, having been too busy not studying for the English final to pay decent attention to not studying for this one. I chewed on my pen and listened to the clock tick as I made my guesses about events in history. If I didn't decide soon whether to go be a model or stay in school flunking finals, the decision would be made for me. When the bell rang to end first period, I checked my wallet. Yes, there was twenty-seven dollars in it; I could get a round-trip train ticket for sure. So that wouldn't settle it for me. Something had to.

On the way out of the classroom, I grabbed Jade. "My phone died," I told her. "Did you get my messages?"

She stared at my fingers on her sleeve until I let go. "What did you do to yourself?" she asked.

I forced myself not to touch my hair. "I needed a change."

"You look like a freak," she whispered. "And when we

text, I would appreciate it if you didn't copy it to every person in your contact list."

"What?" I yelled. "I didn't!"

She was walking away, with Serena following. Serena daringly turned around fast and mouthed, "Yes, you did!"

Then, with a quick glance at Jade, she dashed back to me and held up her phone. On it was a text from me to her:

Roxie Green is a jealous slut.

I just stood there with my mouth hanging open.

"Allison?"

I turned around. It was Tyler. I walked away from him.

"Hey," he said. "Wait up!"

I didn't. I kept walking. I walked right out of school.

He followed me. "Where are you going?"

"Train station," I called back, over my shoulder.

"Why?" He had caught up to me.

"To be a model," I said, without looking at him.

"Oh," he said.

"You'll be late for second period," I said after a few moments.

"Yeah," he said. He touched my hair near the back of my neck with his fingertips.

"What?" I asked.

"Fierce," he said.

"I'm thinking of bleaching it," I said.

"Cool," he said. "Um, I got your text."

Fantastic, I thought. *Why don't I chop my own head off?* "It wasn't intended for you," I said.

"Oh," he said. "Roxie was pretty devastated. . . ."

"She got it too?"

He nodded.

"About her being jealous?"

"'Jealous slut,' I think was the phrase."

"My phone is possessed."

"You mentioned that."

We walked awhile without talking, until I stopped in front of him. "Look," I said. "I know what happened Saturday night."

"What happened?" he asked, all innocent, but he blushed deep red. That was all the proof I needed.

"Please," I said. "It's fine, you don't owe me anything, we're not going out or anything, though she is going out with your best friend, which is kind of lousy of you both, by the way."

"Allison, that's completely—"

"But would you please do me the favor of not trailing me around town? I have a train to catch." I sounded so like my mother I almost smiled, so I quickly pivoted and walked away.

He caught up again.

"Roxie is my friend, too," he said. "She's physical; she's flirty. That doesn't make her a slut. I wasn't hooking

210

up with her; we were just hanging out."

"Right."

He grabbed my arm. "You're right, okay, I know we're not going out. But you are, like, the hottest girl I know, and I can't tell if you like me or hate me or what."

We stood there on the sidewalk, facing each other. I came up to his neck. It was a nice neck, and I noticed he had sort of puffy lips, nice ones. "I'm what?"

"Hot," he said. "Totally hot. And kind of a bitch."

I thought about that for a few seconds.

"What?" he asked.

"It's easier to believe the bad part."

"They're both true."

I felt a weird bubble of giggles rising again. "Wait a sec," I said. "You like me because of how I look?"

He shrugged. "That's part of it. What?"

"It's just so funny."

"Why?" he asked, reddening again. "Were you interested in me, if you were, because of my deep intellectual or philanthropic virtues? Or because you liked how I look?"

"Your vocabulary," I said.

"Well, some of us are shallow. What time's your train?"

"I don't know," I admitted.

We started walking again, and as we rounded the corner by the train station, he asked, "So you really are a model?"

A train was pulling up. I started to run for it and he ran with me. "I have no idea," I said. I took the stairs two at a time and got into the train before the doors closed.

"Good luck," he said.

"I'll need it." The doors closed. He might have been saying, *No, you don't,* but I couldn't be sure. I slumped down in my seat and concocted excuses about my grandmother or an internship in case the conductor demanded an explanation for why I was on the train during school hours. The only thing he asked me for was my money, plus the extra for buying my ticket on the train.

I tried to find the subway I'd taken with Roxie, but there were so many people going in so many directions I ended up standing still and getting spun around like a kid wearing a blindfold in Pin the Tail on the Donkey. *Great,* I was thinking. *I'll just spin here until I'm dizzy and then crawl on home.* I took out my phone to check the time and before I remembered that my phone was dead, I saw that it wasn't. It was alive and fully juiced, with one text message. It was from Quinn.

Where r u?

As I stood there getting jostled and trying to decide what to text back, the phone rang in my hand.

"Hello?"

"Change of venue," the vaguely British, possibly male voice said. "There was an elevator disaster and obviously Filonia won't walk up stairs."

"Oh," I said.

"Are you writing this down? You need to go to Filonia's studio. Do you have that address?"

"No," I said.

He sighed and told me an address.

"I'm at Grand Central," I said, faking Mom's take-charge manner. "What's the best way to get there?"

"Take a cab," he said. "Or else the shuttle to the 1 to Christopher . . ."

"I'll take a cab," I said. "Thanks." He hung up before I could ask how much he thought it would cost.

After wandering around and getting distracted by the amazing painted ceiling for a little while, I found my way out to a taxi line and, when I got in the cab, told him the address. Off we went, like this was a totally reasonable thing for me to be doing.

It took about a half hour of beeping and jolting. Twice I almost threw up, but finally we got there. Wherever *there* was. Filonia's studio. I paid the driver with a ten and he didn't give me any change even though the meter said only $9.70. *Whatever. Keep the change.*

He peeled out as I was slamming the door.

I pushed the button next to the Filonia Studio. It was only one thirty but I was scared to just wander around. My stomach growled, but I didn't think I could very well plop down on the sidewalk and eat my lunch there. The door buzzed loudly. By the time I realized I was supposed to pull it, it had stopped buzzing and I had to press the button again.

In the tiny elevator going up to the fourth floor, it hit me that I probably should have worn some makeup. Then the door slid open and there was no turning back.

22

A SHORT WOMAN DRESSED all in white frowned at me. "You can put your clothes over there," she said, gesturing to a chair and walking away. The room was all white, too, but filled with lights, clamps, and props like a large ceramic banana and a wall full of hats on hooks.

"My what?" My entire body started shaking. "Put my what?"

"Clothes," said a girl in jeans and a black T-shirt, who seemed to materialize out of nowhere. She was pointing at my backpack. "Why don't you unpack and let Filonia see what you brought?"

"I brought my books," I said.

They stared at me.

"Was I supposed to bring other clothes?"

"Are you here for the modeling shoot?" the woman in white said. "Or are you the delivery girl?"

I wasn't sure, so I just stood there and tried not to cry.

"Are you Alison Avery?" The girl in the jeans was reading off a large index card. I nodded. "I'm Seven," she said. "Come with me and we'll do your makeup."

"You're what?" I asked, following her. My mother would kill me, I was thinking, and she would be totally right.

"That's my name," the girl said. "Seven. Sit right here and let's take a look." She turned a light on and looked at my face.

"Your real name?"

"It is now," she said. "I chose it."

"Oh," I said, feeling oddly relieved that this stranger hadn't just had uninterested parents who gave their kids numbers instead of names. Why that would matter to me was, at that point, beyond my ability to even wonder.

She took some cream and rubbed it between her hands. "The last girl came with full makeup. Can you believe it? Where do they get these rubes, you know? Did she think she was going to her prom or something? Can I clean up your brows? You've got some stragglers."

I didn't really answer, just kind of grunted, and felt her yank hairs off my face.

"I like your hair," she said. "Where'd you get it cut? Astor Place?"

"Willow Street," I said truthfully.

She shrugged and started brushing powder over my forehead. "It's easier for some people to change their minds than their hair, you know?"

I smiled. It was weirdly relaxing having her work on my face.

"But I work with these kids, at Sloan? They're in the chemo ward, right, so they have no hair? But I go in Sundays, and you know, they are so sweet, those little girls. I mean, they have no eyelashes, most of them, so mascara is out, but they love the lipstick, I tell ya."

"You volunteer in the cancer ward?" I asked.

"Yeah," Seven said. "I figure everybody should get to feel gorgeous, you know? A little lipstick, some blush . . . gives us something to hide behind and then, whoosh, out comes our beauty, right? Close your eyes."

I closed my eyes. She brushed mascara over my lashes, with a slight jiggling movement at the start of each stroke. Kids with cancer. Now on top of feeling crappy about myself for all the terrible stuff I'd done, I also had to come face-to-face with the obscene grandiosity of my petty self-loathing. I had a hell of a nerve bemoaning my fate when the last girls getting made up by Seven had *no eyelashes*. Is it possible to hate yourself more than completely?

"And these kids," Seven was saying, "oh, they kill me. One girl, this girl Lisa? She always wants smoky eyes. So cute. Okay, you're good."

"I'm what?" I asked.

"You want a natural look for these," Seven said, then leaned close and whispered in my ear, "Don't let Filonia scare you. She's amazing, the best, right? Go ahead. Good luck. You've got the look, that's for sure. Nico should be here for the interview; I don't know where he is, but I'll stick around in case you start getting shiny, no worries."

"Can we go?" Filonia barked from the other room.

I stepped out and she looked me up and down. I may have smelled bad, because her nose twitched a little. "What else did you bring?" she asked.

"Biology textbook?"

A guy walked in holding a tray of coffees. Nobody seemed to notice him.

"Why are you wearing red?" Filonia asked me.

"Um," I said. Filonia crossed her arms and waited. "Because my best friend fooled around with my crush?"

The guy laughed. Filonia rolled her eyes. "Nico, make yourself useful, would you?"

I couldn't help noticing that Nico's haircut looked a lot like mine.

"You want me to interview her while you shoot her?" Nico asked. Nobody answered. I assured myself that nobody was going to shoot me with bullets, just cameras. At that point, I wasn't sure which would be my preference, given the choice.

Filonia blew air from her lips up to her hair. "Clothes," she said to me. "That's all you brought?"

I nodded.

She clucked her tongue. "Sit," she said. I turned to

where she was pointing, a metal stool across the room. Filonia muttered to herself, clamping cords on lights. She held a black thing the size of my cell phone right in front of my face, clicked a button, looked at it, scowled, and repeated a few times.

I was obviously doing it all wrong already. Then things got worse.

Why? Well, for one thing, she was taking pictures of me. How had I forgotten that having my picture taken, even a snapshot with my sisters or on my birthday as a little kid, had always sunk me armpit-deep in despair and self-loathing? And this was more than a snapshot. She must have taken, like, a thousand shots.

That was the good news, I told myself—out of a thousand pictures there's got to be a good one, right? Even the Fascist would look good in one out of a thousand, especially shot by (supposedly) the best photographer in all of New York City.

The bad news was pretty much everything else. The girl who was there just before me was much better. She really knew how to do it, according to Filonia. She had so much energy, that other girl; she was alive in every picture. I, apparently, was dead. The girl Friday afternoon, Filonia called to Seven and Nico—what was her name? Siddhartha. She was wild. They all exchanged knowing glances, and murmured things like "accessories" and "spicy" and then laughed happily together while I shrank on the stool.

But that's not all. Apparently the spaces between my fingers are frighteningly pale. Filonia needed Seven to put makeup on them because they were wrecking the pictures. Oh, joy, the one aspect of myself I had never thought of obsessing over, the spaces between my fingers and their pallor. Also my knuckles were red. (You'd think they could get together with the spaces right there beside them and do a little pigment barter, but no.)

"Your hair looked better a minute ago," Filonia said at one point. Seven didn't come to fix it, and I didn't know how my hair had changed in the past minute, so I smooshed it, trying to get it to revert to whatever it had just stopped doing, but then Filonia said, "No, you're making it worse. Why didn't they tell you to get highlights? Dull, dull, dull. Now, try not to blink so much."

I became a blinking machine. I had never before in my life been so aware of my blinking, and suddenly I couldn't keep my eyes open for more than three seconds at a go. It gave the room a strobe effect, and I started to run a serious risk of falling off the stool.

"Why are you moving that way?"

"Can I stand up?" I asked.

"Just try to smile naturally," she instructed.

I could not summon a single muscle memory of how my face normally smiled. Had I ever smiled normally in my life? Filonia sighed and stepped away from her cameras.

"Let's try something else," she said. She set up a chair with a table in front, hoisted my backpack on top, and told me to sit down and lean forward over it. I didn't know exactly what she meant to do, but I tried and, shockingly, did not succeed.

"Look a little more left and a little more right," she said.

So I crossed my eyes. She snapped the picture.

"Can you do something more *fun* with your left hand?" she asked, causing my left hand to feel as if it were magically growing to twenty times its normal size and weight. I could barely lift it. The one fun thing I could think of to do with it would have been rude. I splayed the fingers on it out, which caused a whole pale-spaces emergency again.

When that was resolved, I propped my head up on top of my backpack. Filonia snapped a few halfhearted frames. "Turn." I turned. "No, the other way. Your nose starts right up by your forehead on that side."

I didn't ask where it started on the other side, just turned my head and tried in vain to stop blinking.

"Don't do so much of that," Filonia instructed. "What you were doing just now. Maybe a little more something else. Now you're blinking again."

"I can't . . ." I started, and then stopped and tried to smile naturally.

"What's wrong?" she asked.

"I don't know how to do this," I said.

"Do what? Just relax."

"I'm not sure why I'm here. I don't even like to have my picture taken and I am obviously bad at it and I should be in English class and my mother is going to kill me."

All three of them started reassuring me that I was doing a great job. Which made it that much worse.

"No, I'm not," I insisted. "It's okay, I'm not as spicy and not as energetic, not as alive as those other girls. Fine, I get it. I have pale spaces and red knuckles and too-dark hair and a nose that starts in the wrong place and an oddly unwitty left hand."

Nico laughed, one loud, barking laugh. Then Filonia and Seven cracked smiles, too. Great, that helped, everybody laughing at me. I sniffed, and realized I'd been crying. I wiped my face, and my mottled, ill-humored left hand came away streaked with mascara. Seven darted forward with a makeup sponge but Filonia stopped her. "Hold it," she said, and came in close with her camera, snapping away. I didn't even care at that point, didn't bother with a fake smile. I just looked at her through her camera and thought about how much I hated her right then. *So what if I'm not pretty*, I thought. *Screw you. This is who I am. You want a picture of a mess? Snap away.*

After a few minutes, she stopped and stood up.

"Good," she said.

"Can I go now?"

"That was excellent," she said, looking at her screen.

"You have some talent after all." Then she turned around and went to fuss with her cameras, saying, "All yours, Nico," as she bent down to unclamp something.

I sniffed again and looked over at Nico, who was staring at me with a slight smile on his stubbly face. He took out a notebook and gestured for me to come to him.

I grabbed my backpack and trudged over. When I sat down, Seven came by and wiped a soft sponge over my face and whispered, "That was great, Allison."

"Sorry," I said.

"Funny career choice for someone who hates having her picture taken," Nico said. "You mind?" He indicated a recorder on the table between us. I shook my head and he turned it on.

"Have you always wanted to model?"

"Never," I said.

He smiled. It was a nice smile, friendly, a little crooked, like Tyler Moss's.

"I have to ask you these questions." He held up a pad. "I'll be quick, okay?"

"Okay."

"Do you play any sports?"

"No. Tennis," I said. "I used to."

"Why'd you stop?"

I shrugged.

"Okay, um, any hobbies?"

I tried to think of a hobby. What kind of a person has

no hobbies? A pale-fingered oddball. "No."

Any siblings?"

Phew! At least I had something. "Two sisters," I said.

"What are they like?"

"They're great."

He made a *go on* movement with his hand.

I sighed. "The older one, Quinn, is brilliant—straight A's, plays piano, never does anything bad. The younger one, Phoebe, is beautiful, sweet, nice, popular, the luckiest person ever. And then there's me, trapped between them."

"Trapped?" Nico asked.

"Middle child," I said, checking the time on my cell. "You know."

He nodded. "And parents?"

"Yes. Two."

He smiled. "What do they do?"

"Oh, my dad is a kindergarten teacher. He's really nice, nicest guy in the world, everybody says, mellow, steady. My mom is a . . . well, she was a hedge fund manager."

"Was?"

"She got fired."

"That must be hard for you," Nico said.

"No," I started to say.

He tilted his head, interested.

"I mean, sure, a little." I felt like I might start bawling again, so I didn't say any more. What a head case.

"So why did she get fired?"

"I don't know. But, hey, can you, like, not use that? It's kind of private, so can you erase that part?"

"No worries," Nico said. "I was just curious. They'll edit it down to ten words or so at most, or nothing. You know."

Ah, I realized. They'd only use any of the interview stuff for the *winner.* He just had to go through the motions. I nodded.

Backtracking from what he could see I had just figured out, he politely added, "It's just a part of the thing, you know, pro forma, make it legit, for the ten K for the scholarship. You know."

I nodded, unsure and not really caring, but I didn't want to seem like more of an idiot than I already felt like. "Whatever."

"You know what?" he said softly. "You don't have to tell me what happened at her work. This is about you. How did her getting fired affect you?"

"It didn't," I said, blowing it off. "I mean, it's not like we lost our house or anything, though who can tell the future, you know? We might."

"Really? You might lose your house?"

"I don't know. I know they're worried about it."

"It's a big thing these days," Nico said quietly. "A lot of families are losing their houses, with the whole mortgage fiasco."

I shrugged. "Yeah, well, they aren't really telling us anything, so we just have to let our imaginations get the best of us, you know?"

"Scary." He wrote something down on his pad.

I didn't want him to pity me, write down that I was some fragile head case. So I quickly backpedaled. "But what I mean is, money is just money. Losing it isn't like getting a terminal disease. It's easy to feel sorry for yourself, feel like everybody else has it better, easier, more glamorous. But you have to remember how good you have it. I'm, like, the queen of feeling sorry for myself, but even I have to have some perspective."

He was nodding and leaning forward like I was so wise and deep, I couldn't stop myself from spouting more of my beautiful bullshit philosophy that I wished I believed in.

"People in my town get so hung up on surfaces, what they have, what they look like. I mean, come on. I just don't care, is the thing. It's scary, I guess, the whole crazy, like, economy thing, but my family is strong. We'll just hang together through whatever happens. Like, I can't go to Tennis Europe this summer, but so what? In the scheme of things. Actually, to tell the truth, I was kind of relieved about that."

He let out a little sigh-laugh and said, "I hear you. I got sent to California on a Teen Tour back in the day. Let me tell you."

I nodded. "Exactly. So, I actually count that as a plus.

I'm happy to just hang around and swim, veg out."

He laughed again, then asked, "You swim?"

"Not like on a team. More like, I lie on a raft in our pool."

"Now there's a team I could've started for—raft lying."

"Yeah, me too," I said. "Well, if we still have a pool. I just focus on getting through the day, at this point."

He chuckled and then asked me about my favorite color (black), my favorite music (anything by bands with colors in their names), favorite food (gummy bears), my hero (Gouverneur Morris), how would I describe my style.

"My style?" I asked.

He winked. "It's a fashion magazine. Remember?"

"Right," I said. "Um, neo-post-middle-school?"

He cracked up.

Then he thanked me and turned off the tape recorder just as the door buzzed—and so did my phone.

23

IT WAS A TEXT FROM QUINN:

Where the f. r u?

I was just texting her back when my phone rang. It was Mom.

"Where the hell are you?"

I smiled instinctively at the family resemblance, and then felt my stomach clench. "Um," I said. Six wise-guy answers popped into my head, starting with, "Getting out of an elevator," but I squelched them. I had at least that much survival sense.

"Are you at school?" Mom asked.

"No. Mom, please don't freak out. . . ."

"Too late," she growled.

"I'm in the city, and I—"

"She's in the city," Mom said to somebody. "Where?"

I looked for a street sign. The sign on the store beside me offered tattoos or *Any body part "pierced," $15.* "Um," I said. "I'm at . . . the corner of . . ." I was walking fast away from the tattoo parlor, passing a shop that sold only condoms, apparently, past another selling whips, chains, and T-shirts printed with stuff you'd probably be suspended for thinking about in my school, and then a Duane Reade drugstore and a bank. "MacDougal and West Third?"

"She's in the Village," Mom said. "Is there a Starbucks?"

I looked around. Across the street was a store all boarded up and a creepy-looking store that advertised *All VHS discount $9* and also *Live Girls*. I tried to reassure myself that live was better than dead, but that just made me feel very young and very suburban and also a bit like I was about to start crying again.

"Allison?"

"I'm here," I managed. "Oh, I see a Starbucks. It's on West Third."

"We're coming to get you. South of MacDougal?"

"I don't know." Did she think I had brought a compass? I hadn't intended to go exploring the arctic. In fact, I hadn't intended even to be exploring MacDougal Street.

"We'll find you. Keep your phone on. You are in big trouble, little girl."

"I know," I said.

She hung up. I crossed the street at the light. A girl crossing next to me was holding hands with a guy, and they were laughing like nothing could ever go wrong. I followed them into Starbucks, but instead of trying to be slick I ordered a water and sat down at a table by the window to wait.

After a very long time, or maybe it was only half an hour, I picked up my phone and texted Roxie:

Hey.

She texted back: *Y r u texting a jealous slut?*

Because she is my bff, I texted back.

Hahahahaha, was her reply.

I was mad because u hooked up w Ty Sat nite. I don't even care anymore. I am in a Starbucks in the Village—after the awful callback which I flunked and before my parents come to kill me and I just wanted to say b4 they do that I'm sorry I said that about you, sorry my evil phone sent it to everybody, and that I don't care who you (or Ty) hook up with.

Send.

I waited, sipping the dregs of my water.

I didn't, is all she sent back.

People said you totally did. It's OK.

People lie, she texted back.

Yes, I thought, *I know.* But which people? It's hard to tell which people to believe, and which ones to trust to have your best interests at heart, according to my friend the devil. So how do you know what to think? How do you ever trust anybody? *Maybe the answer is you never should,* I thought, but then immediately another part of me thought, *What kind of life would that be?* Not just bitter

230

but also probably impossible to pull off. At some point you just have to close your eyes and jump. But which way?

True, I texted back.

I like Emmett, and Ty is crazy about YOU, and even if I liked him (which I don't, not that way), why would I do that to my (I thought) bff?

IDK, I said, scrunching down smaller in my chair. A skinny person of uncertain gender asked if he/she could sit in the other chair at my table and I shrugged.

I wdn't, Roxie texted back.

Either Jade is lying or Roxie is lying, I thought, *or else Jade misperceived what was going on. That's possible.* After all these years of being friends with Jade, after so many projects together and shared secrets and sleepovers, I still wasn't sure of her.

I believed Roxie.

The new girl with the bangles on her wrists and the loud, barky laugh who hadn't gotten into any high schools, who I barely knew, who was, yes, physical and flirty, so out there, and who had every reason to be jealous because I had gotten, somehow, the thing she wanted.

I believed her.

Well, then I suck even worse, I texted.

Yes u do, she sent back. *U jump to nasty conclusions and hurt people who r good to u and u better stop it bc I am not the most patient person in the world.*

Yes u r, I wrote. *If u forgive me.*

Allison, u have a gorgeous soul and maybe u don't know it but I do. But at some point I am going to get sick of your shit.

I had to smile, reading that. *I'm done,* I texted back, surprised that I really felt like I meant it.

Good, she texted back. *Where r u?*

Starbucks. MacDougal and W 3rd. Got a water (no more double shots 4 me) and waiting for my parents to come rip my head off. Uh-oh, here they r. Wish me luck.

Luck, she texted back as I slammed out the door and headed toward my father's waiting car.

They both stared at me without smiling as I slid into the backseat. I mumbled a "thanks for picking me up" and they both turned around. Dad started driving.

I waited for them to start yelling but they didn't. Once we hit the highway, Mom asked, without turning around, "What happened to your hair?"

"I cut it."

"Who did?"

"I did it myself," I said.

"Where?"

"At home," I answered. "In my bathroom. Do you like it?"

"No," she said.

After that, they said nothing else, just stared out the front window, and I stared at the backs of their heads for the next hour, as we drove home.

When we made the turn into our development and

passed the Magnolia Estates sign, Mom turned around and looked at me. "When we get in the house, you will say hello to your sisters, who are worried sick about you, and then go directly to the study, where we will discuss what in the hell is going on with you."

I nodded, and closed my eyes. I knew we were home when I felt the car turn sharply left and then tilt, going up the driveway. I got out of the car first and heard their footsteps behind me on the walk.

The door flew open. It was Phoebe, with Quinn right behind her, and Gosia a shadow behind them. Phoebe threw her arms around me as she tumbled out onto the steps in her socks, and whispered, "They were more scared than mad. Don't worry. Are you okay?"

"I'm fine."

Quinn hugged me next and whispered, "I tried to get you all day! I said you probably went over to a friend's but . . ."

"It's okay," I said.

Gosia hugged me, handed me a plate with a cut-up apple and some cheese, and whispered, "Your favorites."

I didn't get to thank her because I saw Mom standing with her arms crossed, waiting for me to go to the study. I took the cheese and apple in with me so Gosia's feelings wouldn't be hurt, wondering if that's really why she always made that for me. All this time I thought she just gave Phoebe a cookie because she liked me less. Had I once told her that I liked apple and cheese for a snack? It sounded actually kind of familiar.

Just what I needed to be figuring out, right? I sat down on one of the chairs and set my untouched plate on the table beside me. The antenna of the baby monitor was just visible over the rim of the garbage basket. Mom and Dad sat down on two other chairs, facing me.

I waited for them to start.

"We have two or three questions for you for now," Dad said. "We want you to answer truthfully, because our trust in you has been severely shaken, and that is the most disappointing part of all this."

I clenched my jaw tight and reminded myself that even if they both hated me, at least one person, Roxie Green, thought I was worth a third chance.

"Why did you leave school today and go into the city, despite everything that happened last week, and giving us your word it wouldn't happen again?" Mom asked quietly, her hands laid lightly on the arms of the chair and her face serious.

I took a breath and tried to decide how far back in the truth to start. "I was never chosen for anything before."

"I'm asking about your choice to—"

"I know, Mom, and I'm trying to answer honestly."

She sat back in her seat and they both listened (and, I assumed, my sisters upstairs listened) as I explained slowly and carefully about getting to be friends with Roxie, and selling my cell phone to the devil, and that I was pretty sure but not certain that the devil was just a dream. They seemed convinced about that interpretation. I went through the whole thing, everything that had happened (well, I left out the actual kissing Tyler part) up to and including the text that got sent to my entire contact list.

"Yes, I got that text," Mom said.

"Me, too," Dad said. "I wondered what that was about."

"I figured it was probably for the best," Mom said. "She didn't seem like a very good influence. I kept waiting for you to tell me why you sent that to me."

"If I say the devil made me do it, will you get mad and think I am for once trying to be cute?"

Mom's lips pursed; Dad's face regained its seriousness.

"Well, anyway," I said, "that's what happened, and I needed to just get away from everybody for a little while, so it seemed like an omen that I should just go to this appointment and see what it was like."

"And what was it like?" Dad asked.

"Embarrassing."

The lines on his forehead deepened. "Why?"

"You know how I am, getting my picture taken."

He smiled a tiny bit. "Did they hurt you in any way?"

"Just my pride," I said. "Which is kind of overly fragile anyway. As you also know. It was stupid. I admit that. I know I was stupid to go, because you didn't know where I was and it wasn't safe and also because it was stupid to think I could be pretty enough to be in a magazine. There's no reason you should believe me this time, so you can punish me any way you want, and I wouldn't blame you if you did. But I swear I won't be going into the city again; I won't be taking any more stupid risks. I'm done trying to convince myself I'm somebody. I've learned my lesson and I'm ready to crawl back into my hole."

My parents both sat there and stared at me for so long, I started to sweat. I looked down at my hands, watching my fingers grip one another. When I heard a short sniff I looked up. It was my father, who had a tear running down his face.

"You are so wrong, Allison."

"I'm sorry," I said. *What a jerk I am*, I was thinking. *I made my father cry. What a colossal screwup disaster disappointment I am.*

"You're not pretty," he said.

Rub it in, I was thinking, though also, *He has a right, I suppose.*

"Pretty is . . . pretty is like *nice*. It's small. It's pleasant," he said. "If that's what you were aiming for, Allison, you were doomed from the start to abject failure. Your looks are the least of you but— Stop, please don't interrupt to agree with me, Lemon; let me tell you what I can't believe you don't know. You are magnificent. Your personality, your smarts, your humor, and your fighting spirit are all so impressive to us—and yes, sometimes humbling for us to handle as parents, but how you look? Allison, your beauty continues to shock me every day of your life, from the moment you were born and I looked at your wide almond eyes that had an ungodly ability to focus on mine, to this instant as you sit there in front of me. Your soul comes through your face like nobody's I've ever known—your vulnerability and cocksure confidence, your independence and fragility—they shine through your eyes, your mouth, your body. You were a child people's eyes were drawn to, and you are becoming a woman nobody can look away from. Pretty? Allison, you are gorgeous."

Tears were running down my face by then as well, and Mom's.

"I am so sorry that you don't know that."

My phone buzzed in my pocket. "I think that's the devil letting me know his side of the deal is done now," I said, and tried to laugh, to show it was a joke. They didn't laugh, and I didn't reach for my phone, which, thankfully, shut up.

Mom told me they were going to have to talk about where to go from here, but that for now I should go up to my room. I stood up and said okay and headed for the door.

Dad stepped in my way and gathered me in for a hug. Mom hugged me from the other side and, kissing my head, whispered, "I just love your thick, wavy hair so much, Allison. But this is sharp. I might just take a while to get used to it. But Daddy is right. . . ."

"It's okay, Mom," I said, and wiggled away from them. I dashed out and took the stairs two at a time, suddenly desperate for the cool feel of my pillows against my hot face.

I didn't wake up until morning, having slept for twelve dreamless hours.

24

I WOKE UP TUESDAY INTENDING to confront Jade about why she would lie to me about Roxie. I tried to work myself into a fury as I messed with my spiky hair in front of the mirror: *This is it,* I kept saying to her in my mind. *I can never be your friend again. No matter how cranky or difficult I have ever been, how tough it has been to put up with moody me all these years, I have never lied to you, never done anything even close to this betrayal.* I went over it so many times, it was rubbed sharp and deadly, a perfect and irrefutable argument that would, and should, destroy Jade.

But by the time I was heading toward the bus, I felt done already. Maybe I was just tired. As the bus sloped down the hill toward her stop, I thought, *Okay, here we go.* She and Serena sat down in the seat in front of me, their heads bent together, whispering.

Maybe she misinterpreted what she saw, I told myself. Maybe she wasn't trying to make up something that wasn't

239

there; she just saw Roxie behaving in a way that seemed obviously slutty and out-of-bounds to her, and she honestly wanted to protect me. Or maybe she was trying to turn me against Roxie because she didn't want to lose my friendship.

Whatever. I didn't say anything. I just let it slide. For once it wasn't because I was afraid of making Jade angry or disappointed at me. I kind of felt bad for her, a little, and maybe also beyond it.

I walked around school much looser all day, saying hi to people, even smiling occasionally. Maybe it was less humid or the pollen count was down, something like that. Or maybe I had just hit the point where I was over Jade's shit.

That was the one scary thing I did on Tuesday—because not confronting Jade kind of felt like letting that friendship go.

My math final was actually easy. As I wandered down the hall after it, I texted everybody in my contact list a correction:

About what I said Sat night about Roxie Green? I mistyped. What I meant to say was that Roxie Green is an amazing friend and the most fun person I've ever met. I regret the error. Love, Alison Avery

It was weird how many people texted back stuff like, *you are an amazing friend too*, or, *whatever you say—do you guys*

240

want to come over for a pool party Sat nite?

I had decided to crawl back into my hole, but I couldn't seem to find it. As gorgeous as the weather was, mid-eighties with low humidity, even that wasn't pissing me off.

When Susannah Millstein asked what I was doing over the summer, and I told her I didn't know, mostly hanging out, she smiled and said she had gotten her parents to let her pull out of Tennis Intensive at Duke University to have some downtime. She asked if maybe I'd like to hang out some, and when I said sure, I actually meant it.

Weird.

Seventh period, when I explained to my English teacher, Mr. Katz, that I had needed to leave school early the day before for, um, personal reasons, he got all flustered and said no problem, and let me take the final out in the hall while the class watched a movie version of *Candide* all period. When the bell rang, I handed in my bogus essays along with my autobiography in six words:

Sold my cell to the devil.

He laughed out loud. "Like Faust, but your cell instead of your soul?" he asked.

"Um, yeah," I answered, remembering the name vaguely from something we were supposed to have read.

"Excellent. Well, I hope it works out better for you than him."

"Jury's still out."

* * *

I performed my Gouverneur Morris thing for the assembly Wednesday, and got an honorable mention. It would have been nice for once to be the winner, but what did I really expect? Anyway, there was a certificate. I put it on the counter when I got home and waited to see if anybody was going to magnet it to the fridge.

Thursday morning, there it was, amid the forest of my sisters' test papers and commendations.

Embarrassingly, it mattered a tiny bit to me, as stupid as that is. Still, it was the one thing I'd actually worked on all year, so, whatever.

Anyway, it kind of cracked me up all morning, in and out of my last finals, thinking how proud I was to have a crappy sheet of paper on the fridge with my name Sharpied in on the (name) line, and that's why I was apparently smirking as I walked with Roxie out to the field at lunch.

In answer to Tyler's question.

But I didn't answer. I just shrugged, and then he asked if he could talk to me. My fingers went icy as I walked with him toward the back fence.

I hadn't really spoken to him since getting on the train Monday morning, had avoided him pretty much, because I figured, now that I had put the word out that no, I was not a model, that some rumors actually are false, he wouldn't have much use for me. And since I was done humiliating myself—had determined, in this last week of school, to turn over a new leaf and not walk face-first into windmills—there was no reason to cross paths with Tyler Moss if I could possibly avoid it.

It wasn't just "honorable mention" on the social studies presentations I was busy congratulating myself about. I was feeling pretty proud of my newfound self-preservation instinct.

"You don't have to say anything," I told Ty, feeling way impressed with my own maturity. "It's okay."

"What's okay?" he asked. He was all kind of blotchy and nervous-looking, poor thing.

"You were briefly, whatever, into me—if you were—under false information. You thought I was a model. I'm not; I never was. So you don't owe me an explanation or whatever. It's been fun, the end. Let's not drag it out, right?"

I held out my hand to shake his, half joking, to ease the awkwardness. He was a good-looking, sarcastic jock; I was a gawky, intense girl who briefly had delusions of grandeur. There really was no reason for us to waste more of each other's time.

"I never hooked up with Roxie Green, if that's what you still think," he said.

"No," I said, and decided to just be blunt. I was hungry and my lunch period was only forty-three minutes long. "Ty, let's be real. You even admitted it—you like me because of how I looked, and that I was a model, but that

243

was all a fake; it never really happened. Tomorrow's the last day of school and we won't see each other all summer. So let's just leave it as acquaintances, right?"

Ty looked at his sneakers. "Okay, I like you because of how you look; it's true," he said. "I'm sorry if that's shallow, but I do; I can't help it."

"It's not that it's shallow," I tried to explain. "It's just—"

"Yeah, but," he continued, kind of ignoring me, "I also like you because you're funny and weird, and every time I'm with you, you surprise me, and also because your hero was, what did you say? 'A one-legged drunken carouser who in spite of his own bad impulses managed to write the most important and generous document in history.' Right?"

"I can't believe you remembered that."

He shrugged. "A one-legged gorgeous girl swinging a plunger in the corridor is pretty memorable. What?"

I just shook my head. "I don't get it."

"What's to get?" He smiled halfway, crooked. "Those are the three things anybody would look for in a girlfriend: hotness, humor, and a kick-ass hero."

I managed not to ask, *Did you just say the word* girlfriend*? Because I think you said* girlfriend, by asking, instead, and randomly, "Well, who's your hero?"

"My brother, Gideon," Ty said without a moment's hesitation.

"Your brother?"

"He didn't write the Constitution, I admit, but his smile lights up the world."

"Talk about a kick-ass hero," I whispered.

"Will you go out with me?" he asked me.

"No," I said.

He looked so shocked and hurt, I hurried to explain.

"I'm not . . . It's not that I don't like you," I said.

"Just not in that way?" he guessed wrongly.

"Oh, no," I said quickly. "In that way. Exactly in that way. I've liked you in that way for, like, the whole year."

"So then, why—"

"You just . . . You have this idea of me," I said. "You think I'm, like, cool, or strong, independent. Maybe even, you know, pretty."

"Yeah?"

"But you're wrong," I said. "I'm not. I suck. You are, like, gorgeous and funny and a jock and smart and totally dedicated to your disabled brother. I'm petty and cranky and awkward and weird-looking. All of which you would realize within days, maybe minutes, and then you'd break up with me and I'd have to spend the rest of the summer in a worse funk than I usually am in."

"Way to look on the bright side," he said, smirking a tiny bit.

"The bright side and I don't get along so well."

"Maybe you're wrong," he said. "What if you don't

suck? What if you're actually way cooler than you think, funnier, more gorgeous, more generous? Maybe your one big fault is that you just have no idea how great you are."

I shook my head. "Trust me."

He watched his sneaker kick at the grass. "Fine. Well, whatever. Have a good summer."

"You too," I managed.

He started to walk away, and though my knees were freaking out I managed to stay upright.

A few steps away, he turned and walked backward, saying, "Call me if you realize you're good enough for me. We could have some fun."

I managed a smile and an "Okay," but I didn't mean it. I knew that was something I'd never realize. Maybe he could tell, because he shrugged, like giving up, then turned around and didn't look back.

25

DAD HAD DECIDED WE WERE grilling that night for dinner, so the rest of us were setting the table and making the salad and everything was chaos. Phoebe was drifting around all tan and happy, having spent the morning at her cute boyfriend's mother's nursery repotting plants, and then the afternoon with a bunch of friends swimming together in our pool. Her long blond hair was still damp against her bronze shoulders. Dad kissed her on her head as she stood beside him, holding the platter and humming in her sweet off-key voice.

Inside, while making the salad, Mom asked Quinn how her meeting had gone. I didn't even know she had such an important meeting, she didn't tell me about it, but apparently it was with her advisor to talk about her summer job working in a camp for underprivileged kids. Quinn was all excited about the job. She carried the big wooden bowl out, and Mom had the tongs she'd gotten on a trip last year to India.

I carried the mustard and the vinegar, following them.

Mom interrupted the Phoebe–Dad duet to tell him to listen to Quinn's wonderful story. Dad ate it up. He loves do-gooder stuff like donating and soup kitchens and all that. He asked Quinn a hundred questions and listened carefully to every answer, nodding with such a proud face, casting glances at Mom like, *Isn't she just remarkable, our shining star?*

Quinn stood at the head of the table with her hands on the smooth sides of the salad bowl, talking about how good it felt to be making a difference in the lives of these kids.

I dropped the jar of mustard and it shattered all over the patio.

It was totally an accident. I watched my parents give each other looks and take their deep breaths. Before I could even apologize, my phone rang.

"Saved by the bell," Phoebe whispered, kneeling down with a roll of paper towels. She was just trying to be sweet and helpful, I knew; there was no reason to grunt at her.

Alas.

I recognized his voice immediately. It was the way he said my name, slow and sure, like he knew me better than I was admitting knowing myself, exactly the way he had said it while stretching his long legs out in front of him while sitting on my couch, trading me gorgeousness for my cell phone.

But this time, after my name, even though I didn't answer, he said, "Congratulations."

I, of course, thought he was talking about Tyler asking me out, and/or my self-protectively smart decision to reject him before he could (eventually, inevitably, heartbreakingly) reject me. So I just said, "Thanks."

But the voice said, "You are a finalist."

"In what?"

He paused, then said, "*Zip* magazine. The New Teen."

I stood there blinking (my real talent) while my whole family looked at me like, *What's going on?* Or maybe, *Why are you rudely preempting your sister's beautiful story of altruism?*

"My assistant will text the address and details, but we'd like you to come in for the final shoot and interview, with me, on Saturday. Noon."

"With you?"

"I'm the editor in chief."

"No way."

"Who else would I be?" he asked, and hung up.

I closed the phone.

"Who was that?" Mom asked.

"The devil," I said.

"Allison," Mom said, a warning brewing in her voice. "I asked you a question."

"And I answered," I said. "I'm a finalist in the modeling contest."

Phoebe, gotta hand it to her, immediately jumped around whooping and yelling, hugging and congratulating me, while the other three stood there dumbfounded and kept asking if I was telling the truth.

I assured them I was. Dad turned away to flip the chicken breasts on the grill. Mom, meanwhile, grilled me: what did that mean, what was this magazine anyway, what had I done to make the finals of this competition.

I tried to answer calm, cool, and collected, but it was hard. I was really wishing I could have a minute just to myself to jump around and shriek (or maybe Phoebe could be there, because she was so purely happy for me it was crazy). A finalist? ME? Seriously?

I could tell Mom was trying to get the information largely to avoid the obvious question of *Why would they choose you, honey?*

I answered every question as best I could, and as factually. No, I hadn't done anything more embarrassing than cry, a little, but not (seeing Dad's alarmed face) because of anything the photographer did or asked me to do, just because I felt so inadequate. But my clothes stayed on.

If I won? Well, I said, of course probably I wouldn't win, but if I did, I would get to go to Nice, France, for one week over the summer with one of my parents, all expenses paid, for an extended photo shoot. Mom and Dad glanced at each other and Phoebe sat down, her chin cupped in her fists, watching me like it was a star sighting.

Quinn was still standing there with her hands on the sides of the salad bowl, looking like she'd been painted there by Vermeer.

"And," I said, "if I win, which I probably won't, of course, but if somehow I did? I would win a ten-thousand-dollar scholarship."

Well, that got everybody's attention. They all stared at me.

I smiled and said to Mom, "I'd give it to you. All of it. I'm sure your lawyer could figure out how to transfer it to you. I know times are tough right now, and it would feel great to me to be able to help out."

I think Mom might have misted up, I really do; it was only a second or part of a second, but time almost slowed down, and I watched a small tear form itself in Mom's eye and I swear it was a tear of pride. I really think that I did not make that up afterward to console myself.

Anyway, that possible fraction of a second was interrupted when Dad, the Zen master, kindergarten Teacher of the Year, nicest guy in the world, slammed down his grilling tongs and said, "Absolutely not."

"Absolutely not what?" I asked.

"My daughter is not prostituting herself to—"

"Daddy!" Phoebe interrupted, objecting, but he plowed right past.

"That's right, prostituting herself! What do you think selling your body is called?"

"Jed," Mom said, for once trying to calm him down. The world had flipped in an instant.

"We do not need the money that badly, Claire!"

"That's not the—"

"We can live perfectly well in a small house, without all the tinsel and glitter. I will not pimp out my daughters to chase shallow dreams of fame and fortune; I won't!"

"It's ten thousand dollars, Jed," Mom said. "It is obviously not going to make a dent, and you know it. The ten thousand dollars is far from the point, and it would belong to her, not us! Would you let Allison talk? You and I can discuss this later."

Dad turned back to the grill.

Mom and Phoebe and Quinn turned to me. But I had nothing really to say. My grand gesture, my huge success, wouldn't even make a dent. It was nothing to them. I could never be good enough, even if I won.

I shrugged. "No big deal," I muttered. "Obviously."

"It is, Allison," Mom said, leaning forward and taking my sweaty hand in her cool one. "We're very proud of you. Tell us about this competition. A finalist!"

"No, you're not!" I said. "It won't make a difference anyway, even if Dad let me go and do it. Just forget it. Let Quinn talk more about helping underprivileged children. Then you guys can feel proud."

Dad slammed the grill shut. "You know what, Allison? We do feel proud of that. We feel proud that Quinn is reaching out to other people, trying to make the world a better place, working toward something that is bigger than herself."

"Congratulations," I said to Quinn.

"Jed!" Mom yelled.

Dad took a deep breath. "It's not that we're not proud of you, too, Allison. It's just that you don't need to give us money. Live a good life; be a good person. Money and strutting your body around are shallow goals, too shallow for you."

He wiped his hands on his apron and came toward me, arms outstretched. "Okay, Lemon?"

"No!" I yelled. And I ran away from him. I ran away across the backyard, past the pool, around the tennis court, across the grass, then around the house to the front. I stood at the top of the driveway, looking down it, to where it turned toward the street, and contemplated putting one foot in front of the other and never looking back. Where would I go?

Did I have the courage to run away?

Or even the desire?

Where did I want to be?

The answer was clear to me as soon as I formulated the question. I went in the door near the kitchen and up the back stairs, across the upstairs den to my room, where I stripped off my clothes and curled up tight in my bed.

I woke up knowing that someone was in the room with

me and that it was dark. To my surprise, it was my mother and not the devil.

"When are you supposed to go?" she asked me.

"Saturday at noon," I said. "I'll just call them tomorrow and say I can't . . ."

"You'll do no such thing," Mom said.

I sat up. "But Dad . . ."

"Daddy loves you very much," Mom said. "He feels very protective of you, and, honestly, very angry at me about some money issues that have nothing to do with you but which you brought up unconsciously. But that is not your problem; it's ours."

I rubbed my eyes. Mom was sitting on my couch, where the devil had sat. "Are you really here or am I dreaming?" The question I had never managed to ask him, I asked her.

She laughed. "I'm really here, Allie Cat." She came around and got on my bed, folding her slim long legs under her as she snuggled in. "And I am so proud of you."

I lay down with my back to her and said thanks.

"Not just for becoming a finalist. I didn't know you were interested in modeling."

"Neither did I," I admitted. "Figures the one thing I seem to be good at—"

"You are good at so many things—"

"Stop," I interrupted. "I'm not and it just makes me feel worse if you—"

254

"I didn't mean to belittle your earning power, Allison."

"Alas," I said.

She giggled behind me, then said, "Point taken. But let me tell you this, daughter of mine. I am proud of you for wanting not just to help, but to make money on your own steam. That is a good impulse, and I'm not saying that doing good in the world is anything but great, but there is power to be had in making your own money, and I applaud you for understanding and pursuing that power, as well as for your generosity in offering to share it."

We lay there for a minute before I said thank-you again.

I was just drifting off to sleep when I heard her say, "And I'm impressed that one of those dumb magazines is smart enough to spot a real beauty. We'll show 'em who's gorgeous Saturday at noon, baby."

"Okay," I think I said, or maybe I just dreamed that.

26

LAST DAY OF SCHOOL. *Good-bye, ninth grade, and don't let the door hit you in the butt.* "Tenth grade is better," Quinn assured me on our way to the bus in the morning. We both had our sunglasses on, but still I could tell she was avoiding making eye contact.

"Halle-frickin-luyah," I answered.

She stopped in front of me. "If you would get your head out of your butt for one minute, Allison, you would notice that I am not perfect and you are not the only one with problems."

"I didn't—"

"I'm *interested* in working at this camp. It's not just padding my résumé."

"I never said—"

"You act like everything I do is to torture you, poor Allison, so trapped in the plot of *East of Eden*."

"The *what*?"

"You do," she said. "Do you even realize how self-aggrandizing that is, to act so troubled, so self-loathing—and meanwhile here you are, suddenly America's Next Top Model, and supposedly the hottest guy in *my* grade is all crazy about you, but still everybody is supposed to tiptoe around your fragile ego?"

"If that's tiptoeing I'd hate to see you stomp," I said.

She sighed and turned away, and we continued down the road. "Congratulations, by the way," she muttered.

"Thanks," I said. "Think Dad will let me go?"

"Mom will wear him down."

We stood at the corner, waiting for the bus, not talking. After a while I asked, "You have problems?"

"You don't even want to know," she said.

"Yes, I do. You just seem so perfect. I didn't think—"

"Things are rarely what they seem," she said, and before I could ask her more, Roxie came dashing up asking me about my weird text message to her, and then the bus showed up as I was asking her, "What text message?"

"That you are a finalist in the New Teen contest!" She slid into the window seat. I sat beside her and said I had not texted her anything; I had gotten into a fight with my parents and then fallen asleep.

"So are you a finalist or not?"

"I am," I said. "That's what's weird. I meant to text you, I swear—but I fell asleep before I did it."

"Maybe you texted me in your sleep," she suggested.

"Sleep texting," I said. "Man, I get weirder by the day."

She grinned at that and I grinned back. "You're going to win," she said.

I shrugged. "Speaking of weird."

"No." She looked closer. "Because gorgeous is surface. You, my friend, are beautiful."

We were pulling up to Jade and Serena's stop. Serena was waving at us and doing little jumps in place. Jade was scowling. *Oh, joy.*

Jade climbed up the bus steps first, with Serena bopping behind her, calling my name and saying, "Congratulations!"

"On what?" I asked.

"Being a finalist!" Serena said.

Jade slid into the seat across the aisle from us, and said, "Thanks for letting the whole world know except me," she said.

"I didn't text anybody," I said, but when Serena held up her phone with the proof, I can't say I was completely shocked. "I must have done it while I was sleeping," I argued. "You didn't get one?" I asked Jade.

"You should know," Jade said, leaning across Serena and biting off her words with horrible precision. "You know what, Allison? I don't really care. It's your life. You're obviously determined to screw it up, so good luck to you. I don't know if it's even true that you are modeling. Personally, I doubt it. I mean, no offense, but you're just not that pretty. That's what everybody is saying, so you know. Nobody believes your little lies about winning this contest. Okay? So you're just making a fool of yourself. There. I said it. The truth hurts. You have to be gorgeous to be a model, and even Roxanne is not that gorgeous. Right? She didn't get a callback. But somehow you did? You, with no experience, who never even likes getting her picture taken, who is—let's be blunt—not that great-looking. If that's harsh, well, it's about time somebody said it to your face instead of just behind your back."

I didn't feel like crying. I just felt cold. I didn't interrupt or object, just sat there letting her tear me to pieces as we bumped through our beautifully manicured town toward the last day of school.

And I was thinking about how much easier it was to believe what she was saying about how I looked than what Roxie had said. *They are just two opinions,* I told myself. It's easier to believe the bad stuff, true, but maybe that's not a good enough reason to decide to believe it.

Serena had turned to Jade to try to stop her, but Jade glared at Serena, and Serena sank down to let her continue.

"Come on, Allison. I don't know why you would make stuff up like the devil came to your bedroom and you are out of the bright blue sky suddenly a supermodel. Nobody believes you. Maybe you're psychotic. Maybe you think

259

that telling these outrageous lies is the only way you can be popular. I don't know and I don't care. I can't stop you from humiliating yourself, but I am done letting you humiliate me. I'm not here to be your punching bag."

I saw Roxie's jaw tighten, but I did not need or want her to handle this one for me.

"Listen, Jade," I said. "I am sorry you didn't get my text. I'm sorry everybody else got it, honestly; my phone actually is possessed by the devil, as psycho as that sounds. Not all improbable things are false. But I am not trying to humiliate you, and I don't think you are my punching bag. I never did. The opposite, in fact."

"Could you speak any louder," she snarled. "I think there are some eleventh graders in the back who can't hear your booming insults."

"Fine," I said louder, ignoring the sarcasm that would normally have withered me in my seat. "I'll speak up then. Jade, you have treated me like your annoying and ugly little cousin all year, and I am sick of it. You make me feel like crap about myself. But the truth is, I am not annoying and I am not ugly."

Jade glared at me, then slid her eyes away. "If you say so," I think she muttered.

"I do say so. A person needs her friends to believe in her more than she believes in herself. Not less. A good friend sticks with you even when weird stuff happens—even when *good* stuff happens. But you, Jade

Demarchelier, are a bad friend."

I sat back in my seat. Roxie started clapping. A few other kids in the back clapped, too. I started to sink down in my seat, but then straightened up instead, deciding, *What the hell*, and smiled, not even caring that my lips disappeared.

The rest of the day went along strangely. I had apparently texted some but not all of the people on my contact list, so half the people I knew were offended and the other half thought they were suddenly very close with somebody nearly famous, and kept texting me all through the day to *have a gr8 summer* and crap like that. I was texting under my desk in practically every class. The usual round of hugs and tears that mark the last day of school, at least for the girls, was even buzzier than in past years. Fifth period I got a text from one girl whose name didn't even look familiar telling me that if I won and was therefore in Nice during August, I should plan to stay an extra few days with her family near there. She actually added, *Bonne chance!*

The girls I apparently had neglected to text about my status as a finalist whispered as I came near them and turned away, shrugging as I passed. Luckily I was mostly walking around with Roxie, so I acted like I didn't care. I caught a glimpse of Tyler laughing with a bunch of tenth graders, but he either didn't see me or pretended not to, and when Emmett waved Roxie over, she called out, "I'll text you later," and kept walking with me.

Since report cards are mailed instead of handed out at the high school, the day ended kind of anticlimactically, and when we got on the bus to go home, I slumped against Roxie and moaned, "Half the people here hate me and the other half only like me because they think I'm someone I'm not."

"Well," she said, "you can't have everything. But you can have this. Here." She handed me a box covered in wrapping paper and ribbon. "Happy end of ninth."

"I didn't get you anything."

She waved that off. "I just wanted . . . you know . . . You're a good friend."

I shook my head.

"You are," she insisted. "You made me feel like less of a loser, and if I did the same for you, good. We're great, right? And when you have people that love you backing you up, anything is possible."

"Roxie, I feel like I have screwed up so many—"

"Your cell sucks, but I blame the devil for that. Open it!"

I tore off the wrapping. It was a clay mask from Origins.

"I always use this mask the night before important modeling calls. Gives you a good glow."

I hugged her. We got off the bus and started up the street.

"Any advice you can give me?" I asked her. "I really hate having my picture taken—I feel so stripped down and

262

ugly, and like the camera is a predator . . ."

She laughed her great loud, barky laugh. "Pretend it's a friend. Pretend it's me! Reveal everything. Pretend you are safe, loved, and gorgeous, and you will be."

I nodded and said I would try.

"Call me after," Roxie said, with another hug in front of her huge house. "Hey, Double Shot? Maybe you should use a landline, though."

I laughed and went the rest of the way home alone.

After dinner that night, while Dad was out for a run, I showed my sisters and mother the mask Roxie had given me and we decided to all do it. We washed our faces and slathered the black slime on, cracking up in Mom's bathroom at how hideous we all looked. Then we sat in a row on the chaise longues beside the pool, watching the sun set together.

Nobody was talking for a while and it felt very peaceful, until Mom said, "I have to tell you girls something."

Quinn and I flashed each other a look but said nothing.

"As you know, Daddy and I have been talking to my lawyers about contesting the grounds I was fired on. It's become clear that although I still believe in my heart and soul that I am guilty of nothing worse than making a bad gamble on a good idea, I'm not going ahead with a lawsuit."

Quinn started to object. Mom cut her off. She stood up and paced in front of us, like she was making a political speech to an audience of three.

"I appreciate your support, Quinn. And you, too, Allison and Phoebe. I don't know what I would do without you girls and the strength you give me. The way that you have kept what is going on with me as private as you have, the way you have managed the various losses I know you've borne—Daddy and I are so grateful, and so proud." She straightened up, her posture ramrod straight, almost military, and with the sun setting behind her right shoulder, she could have been a heroic portrait of herself, except for the clay mask on her face and the T-shirt and cutoffs she was wearing.

"Thank you," Quinn whispered somberly. I swallowed my own impulse to crack up.

"I am going to follow your example here, all of you," Mom continued forcefully, as little flakes of clay fell to her feet. "As horrible and scary and humiliating as this is for me, at least we've been able to keep it fairly quiet. So I have decided not to sue for wrongful termination. Fighting would mean gambling on a very unlikely possibility of success, according to my lawyers. So it's not a strategic move anyway, as much as you know I love to fight the good fight. But the deciding factor is that a lawsuit would guarantee that our family situation would be splashed across the pages of the *Wall Street Journal* and possibly the local paper as well. . . . No. I won't put us through that. I think it would destroy me completely if my work situation were taking a terrible toll on you girls. I am so happy you are all handling it so well. Sometimes, I guess, you move on by surrendering. I'm sorry I have let you girls down."

"You haven't," we all said immediately. I had to turn away from her, so I looked at Phoebe, beside me. A tear was streaking a track down her muddy cheek.

"We'll battle back somehow," Mom said. "There's always another tack to take. That's what I think. We're the Avery women. I love my work, but you are my family, my everything."

A chip of clay fell off Mom's forehead and landed on her foot, and she asked, "What was that?"

That was when I lost it. I started giggling, tried to cover it with a cough, and might have succeeded, if I hadn't heard a strangled little sound escape from Quinn. Her mouth was tight but her shoulders were shuddering as she tried to hold in the laughter. Mine were, too, and then squeaky sounds started seeping out of Phoebe, too, until we were overcome.

"What?" Mom asked. "What's so funny?"

We were trying to explain and pointing at her face and our own when Dad came around the side of the house, caught sight of us all there with the black clay all over our faces, and shrieked.

Mom looked at him, then at us, and that's when it

dawned on her. She doubled over laughing. We all ran, howling, for bathrooms while Daddy, bewildered, kept asking what had happened to our faces.

Later, after we'd washed up, revealing our healthy glow, we put on pajamas and wandered back downstairs, not ready to go our separate ways yet. All five of us fell asleep entangled on the couches in the family room, watching TV, and when we woke up at two in the morning and wandered off to our beds, Dad whispered to me, "Sweet dreams—tomorrow, well, today, will be the first day of the rest of your life," editing what he used to say when I was little. I had a jolt of fear, since that reminded me of what was about to happen that day, and I thought I'd never fall back to sleep. I did, though, way easier than I'd anticipated, with the picture of me, my mother, and my sisters cracking up in our hideous masks, and feeling absolutely beautiful together.

27

I WALKED THROUGH THE double-height glass doors on the thirty-fourth floor of the office building, clutching the bag of clothes I'd brought (better prepared this time) and clenching my jaw. I headed down the long hallway, passing huge blowups of past *zip* covers on both sides. They were beautiful. It was like being in a really cool museum. The receptionist, sitting in front of a bronze wall hanging of the *zip* logo, looked me down and up after I told her my name.

"And you are here for?" she asked.

"For . . . I'm a . . . an interview. A finalist," I babbled. "Allison Avery."

"Ah," she said, "yes," and pointed across the room. There was a red leather couch with a long, gangly girl on it already, her slick black hair pulled back from her angular, dark face. I sat down on the other side of the couch. She smiled, revealing the whitest, straightest teeth I'd ever seen, and asked, "You're a finalist?"

"Weirdly enough," I said, and shook her outstretched hand.

"I know what you mean," she said, and I considered feeling horribly offended, in fact was working up to it, when she continued, "I've spent my whole life feeling hideous, like a freak. Apparently the only ones who disagree are these people."

I felt myself smiling back at her, and said, "But you're gorgeous."

"Me? No way," she said. "You are. My own grandmother told my mother not to worry, I wouldn't always look like this."

"Mine said I was *interesting-looking*!"

"Oh, that's awful," she agreed. "I'm Siddhartha."

"Filonia mentioned you!"

"How I knocked over the whole tray of makeup?"

"No," I assured her. "How great you were."

"Allison Avery?" the receptionist called.

"Oh, Siddhartha was here first," I said.

"I don't care," the receptionist answered.

"I'm way early," Siddhartha said. "Nervous. Good luck!"

I doubled back for my bag and to say *thanks* and *you too*; then had to sprint after the receptionist in her stilettos. I tried not to clomp, since our steps echoed in the hallway. At the end, she swung open a frosted-glass door and said my name.

I stopped short in the doorway when the devil himself smiled at me from behind his desk.

"Go in," the receptionist said.

I did.

"It's you," I managed to say.

He stood up and came around the desk, looking at me, and said, "Allison Avery."

"Yes." The door closed behind me. He gestured to a chair in front of his desk. I went to it and sat down, while he leaned against his desk, never taking his eyes off me.

"Do you need a drink of water?"

I shook my head.

Noticing that I was shivering a little bit, he asked, "Too cold for you? These buildings are always over-air-conditioned."

"Usually I'm sweaty," I said.

"Me, too," he said, though he looked so perfect and cool in his linen suit it was hard to imagine he ever over-heated.

"You are a very interesting girl," he said, and then—I guess I looked a little panicked—he patted a paper on his desk. "Your interview gives us a good potential angle."

"Oh?"

He reached behind him and picked up a big glossy photograph. It was a cover of *zip*, one I hadn't seen before, really dramatic-looking; the girl was gorgeous and crying;

I then realized that *The New Teen* was written across the bottom. Then I saw that the gorgeous girl in the picture was me.

I looked at his face when I could tear my eyes away from the image. "I don't get it," I whispered.

"Very timely, as well as quite arresting, obviously."

"What is?"

"The angle."

"I don't . . ." I was staring at the picture again. It didn't look like me, but it did; it was disturbing but kind of beautiful; it was hard to stop making eye contact with the broken, angry, vulnerable girl in the picture, even knowing that she was me.

"Of course you do, Allison Avery," he said. "Don't play dumb; it's unbecoming."

I looked at him again, and he smiled. "The new teen. Coping with her family's slide into poverty. The heartbreak of losing her house, her home, her social standing. Very newsworthy, and of course you photograph magnificently. A little tightness in the lips, which you should work on."

"They tend to disappear," I said.

"Don't let them. After this you'll go down the hall for the shoot, where we'll get some different looks. For the inside. Versatility—sporty, sweet, innocent—but I think this should be our cover look, to give it punch. But first we will need to get more details, of course, fill out the story. That's your ticket to winning."

"No," I said. "I told Nico, that . . . that's private."

He cocked his head. "But that's the story."

I shook my head.

"Allison," he said, "we can't just have a picture of a crying girl with no story. The story makes the picture. It will all, certainly, be in only the best taste. If anything makes you uncomfortable, we won't print it."

"Oh," I said. "Okay."

"The more details you can provide, of course, the more real it will feel to our readers, and the more likely you are to win."

"I thought it was just about how you look in a picture," I said.

He smiled wickedly. "Is anything so simple?"

"I guess not."

"A picture is an invitation, a question mark. Like beauty itself. What is it that makes one person beautiful and another not? Is it a cream, a blush, an arrangement of fabric? A billion-dollar industry, in which I am a cog, insists that it is. Is it anatomy? Symmetry? Or something more ephemeral? Thomas Aquinas, an old buddy of mine, said three things are needed for beauty: wholeness, harmony, and a killer mascara. No, wait, not mascara. Radiance. That's what he said. Radiance. Not a single plug for a brand of concealer from him. And you, Allison Avery, what is your theory?"

I shrugged.

"It's a simple question. Let's say you are our cover girl. What is beauty, to you?"

"Um," I said, thinking, *They didn't say there was going to be a test.* "I guess it is . . . feeling beautiful?"

"Ah," he said. "A tautology. Beauty is feeling beautiful."

"Or that's what it comes from," I said. "You are most beautiful when you feel beautiful."

"Do you really believe that?"

"No," I admitted. "I don't know. That's what I wish were true."

"And yet you manage to feel beautiful," he said. "Despite the fact that like so many other teens in these difficult economic times, your mother has lost her job, you are losing your house, your summer plans have evaporated, your friendships and social standing are under stress . . ."

"No," I said. "I didn't . . ."

"You texted responses to my assistant. We have them on the record."

"I did not."

He held up a typed paper. "I have it all right here."

I stood up. "You can't have texts from me that I never sent you."

He held out the paper. I only glanced at it but saw, highlighted in yellow, the names *Tyler Moss, Jade Demarchelier, Roxie Green, Quinn,* and *Phoebe.*

"No," I said. "You can't use it. No."

"Sit down, Allison. Let's keep chatting."

"No," I said.

"Don't you want to win?"

"Yes," I said. "I do."

"Winning isn't easy."

"I know."

"There are sacrifices we make if we want success. Do you think your mother got to where she got by shying away from a challenge? Do you think any successful person backed down at the first scary obstacle? If you want to be famous, if you want to be *somebody*—and I think you do— there is a cost. You have to put yourself out there."

"Myself is one thing," I said. "This is my family."

He shrugged. "What price beauty?"

"It would destroy my mother."

"It would make you."

I opened my mouth but no words came out.

"Your mother has had her turn," the devil said softly. "It's your turn now. This is your chance, Allison Avery. This picture is gorgeous, and the story is so timely it will catapult you straight into the talk shows. *Vogue* would want it, *Cosmo*, certainly all the other teen rags. We've already leaked the possibility to Oprah; she's drooling. It's happening, Allison. You've got the look, and you've got the story to propel it. If we pierce the veil of privacy, go behind the hedges in the estates of privilege . . ."

"Our hedges aren't even that high."

"Or you can choose to be afraid. You can say no. It is your choice. But let me be clear: If you walk away from this opportunity, another is highly unlikely to present itself."

"But if I'm so gorgeous . . ."

His eyes narrowed. "You make your reputation with every decision, day by day. And if your reputation is that of a gun-shy shirker, thus will you ever be. There is no turning back. Think carefully. The choices we make determine who we are. Who are you, Allison Avery?"

I swallowed hard, trying to think. Picturing myself on covers of magazines, famous, successful beyond my wildest dreams.

"You are poised to live the fantasy," he said. "How many girls would sell their souls for this chance?"

I blinked and felt a smile start on my mouth. "Not me."

"No?"

"I didn't," I said, and pulled my cell phone out of my pocket. "I just sold my cell phone."

His eyes crinkled slightly as he smiled only with them, at me.

"And that has actually kind of sucked. Because it's my connection, my relationships that I sold, wasn't it?"

He cocked his head.

"I'm still not completely convinced that I have a soul," I told him. "But on the off chance that I do, I don't want to sell it."

He picked up the picture of me on the cover of *zip* again. This time he handed it to me. I put my cell phone down on his desk to hold the picture in both hands. It really was a cool picture. I actually looked gorgeous. I had to admit that if I saw that cover on a rack, I'd probably have to buy the magazine.

When I lifted my eyes again, my cell phone was in his large hand.

We stared at each other.

"It's just a dream," I whispered. "Right?"

"No," he whispered back. "Not just."

I looked back down at the picture of me, a picture I was beginning to recognize, now that I had had time to study it: Beautiful. Vulnerable. Me.

What price beauty?

Was it worth breaking my mother's heart? Or would it just be being honest? I hadn't lied, and it was just my story, my opinion. Maybe the devil was right that telling my story would help other people who were having tough economic times or family crises to cope. Maybe I would be doing something good in the world after all. And maybe for once I would be the Avery sister who people knew and noticed.

And nobody was guaranteeing I would win, anyway. Probably I wouldn't, right? That girl Siddhartha out in the waiting room was way prettier. So who cares; take a chance, right?

A chance to what, though?

If this was my chance to do something big, something good, what would that something be, and for whom?

It was my turn; he was right. All I had to offer was my face, my body, my story.

My story.

My soul.

The ripping sound almost surprised me. It was as if my fingers had made the decision before my brain. I tore straight down the center of the photograph, the middle of my face, the most beautiful picture of myself I'd ever seen. When I got to the end, I stacked the two pieces on top of each other and tore them again, and then again, and again. When I was done and held the scraps of myself in my hands, I stopped. I could so easily see myself throwing them right at the devil, just the way I had thrown my paper about Gouverneur Morris at the Fascist, and it would have looked about as festive. Instead I let the confetti of my own image flutter through my fingertips onto his pristine floor.

He watched until the last scrap fell, and then said, "Alas."

"Alas," I agreed. I held out my hand and he gently placed my cell phone in it. I closed my fingers around it. It was cool to the touch. I grabbed my bag and walked through the scraps of me toward his door. When my hand was on the doorknob, he called my name.

I turned around.

"All to protect your family's honor?" he asked.

I shrugged. "That, or just perversity."

He smiled.

On my way down the hall I looked at my cell phone. It wasn't doing anything weird. I scrolled through my contact list, looking at the names. When I came to Ty, I knew what I wanted to do.

Hey, I texted.

When I got to the reception room I wished a terrified-looking Siddhartha good luck. The receptionist lady tried to explain that I had to go to the photo shoot room, but I thanked her and said I was done. As I was strolling through the corridor of gorgeous girls on *zip* covers, a pantheon I'd never join, Ty texted back:

You good enough yet?

I grinned and pushed the button for the down elevator as I texted back:

Yes. I am now. Will you go out with me?

I stepped into the elevator and my phone flashed, *Searching for network.* I waited to feel the crush of panic, but I didn't. I was okay. I looked at my reflection in the burnished silver of the elevator walls and didn't shrink away in disgust. *Gorgeous,* I whispered to my reflection, trying it out and feeling silly. *Beautiful,* I tried, and my reflection looked back at me like, *Well, maybe.*

It wasn't until I got out of the elevator and was crossing

the vast marble lobby that my phone found service again and buzzed with an answer from Ty:

Yes.

Great, I texted back. *Tell Gideon I look forward to meeting him.*

I pushed out through the revolving door and spotted my family waiting for me at the café across the street. Their heads all turned toward me with questions in their eyes. I shrugged and smiled, and they all smiled back.

It lit the world.

I tucked my cell into my pocket and crossed the street toward them.

Acknowledgments

SOME THINGS I NEED TO ACKNOWLEDGE:

No books by me would be possible without Amy, who knows everything.

Thanks go also to Elise and Rachel, who know the Avery family at least as well as I do, and help me figure out how to bring them to life—and to all their lovely, lively colleagues at HarperCollins who turn my manuscripts into books and get them into, as in this case, your hands.

The good people of the Authors Guild, through advocacy and fellowship, are a writer's best friends. The Writer Girls, who meet too rarely for tea and scones, remind me I'm not alone in this. And my buddies who have my back and make me laugh—I'd be lost without you.

Specific thanks go to Francie for taking me with her to work as a pretend assistant and helping me begin to understand the world of hedge funds and what it takes to succeed; to Mary for sharing tireless encouragement, strong opinions, and vital details about business, but most important, for the boundless joy of her friendship; to Becky, Lucy, Sophie, Isaac, Adam, and Emily, for answering my endless questions and just being all-around cool people to hang with; to Magda, who with great grace makes everything run smoothly; and especially to beautiful Trina for living with us last summer and confiding in me, trusting me, and teaching me . . . about being fifteen, and about being independent and vulnerable all at once.

A special shout-out to Zachary's friends, who are now teens themselves: You guys rock.

I hate to acknowledge but must (this being an acknowledgments page) that the two adorable babies I held when I was a new grown-up myself are, shockingly, heading off to college. Sarah and Hannah, you are such strong, smart, funny, creative, and certainly gorgeous women. Go make some noise, some friends, and some trouble.

"Acknowledge" sounds like something a wisdom-averse person would say: *Ack! Knowledge!* This is just something I think we should all, you know, acknowledge.

Finally . . . a person as blessed as I am—surrounded by such wonderful parents, brother, in-laws, cousins, Aunt Tillie, friends, husband, and kids—should really acknowledge her pure dumb luck at every opportunity. Or not. Perhaps she should just shut up or say only, "Pooh, pooh, pooh." If she did, though, people would think her not only ungrateful but also odd. So you see the problem with an acknowledgments page.

As the devil would say, alas.